DOD TAKES CHARGE

Robin David Peacock

Hawkhill Publishing

Text copyright © 2019 Robert Davis Peacock

ISBN 978-1-9993076-1-5

Contents

Map of Dundee drawn by Alexander Nicol Small, aged twelve years, Hawkhill

1. The City Churchs
2. The Town House
3. Couttie's wynd
4. Public Seminaries
5. Police Station and Jail
6. Infirmary
7. Watt Institution
8. The Howff
9. The "Oralis"
10. Mr David's house
11. Dad's house
12. Wee Tam's house
13. Mr Niven's shop
14. Smalls' Bakery (my house)

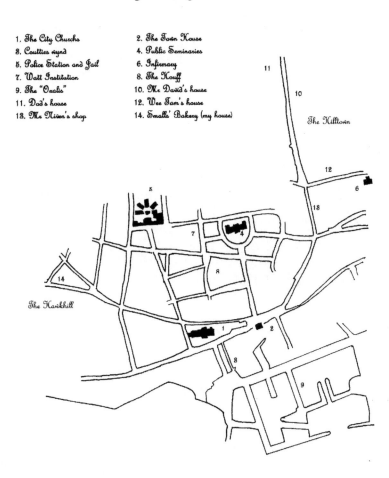

Prologue

Dod was woken by the cold. It was seven in the morning and the fire had probably gone out at two or three o'clock. He couldn't afford to light it until just before his mother returned from work so there was no chance of a cup of tea. He pulled on his trousers, put on his coat, wrapped a muffler round his neck and pulled his cap over his ears. He picked up his notebook and pencil and was about to put them in his pocket when he noticed that the pencil lead was broken. He picked up the bread knife, sharpened the pencil to a fine point, wrapped it in his handkerchief and stuffed it in his coat pocket. He locked the door of the single room and put the key under the mat. A quick visit to the privy outside and he was off into town to try and find breakfast. He had no idea that today, Wednesday the 7th November 1849, would be different from any other day.

Chapter 1

In which Mr Small and Mr David interrupt a
robbery

Dundee in November is dark by the early evening. True, the main streets were now lit by the new flickering gas lights, but they did not illuminate the side streets or the many closes and entries leading off them. Some of the wider of these had a few whale oil lanterns to alleviate the gloom but most were almost pitch dark. You would only go down these dark wynds if you lived there or if you were up to no good.

John Small had just emerged from the Town House where he had been attending a Council meeting. Waiting for him under the Pillars was his friend Peter David. It was a Wednesday evening and the two men customarily met for a drink and a gossip. John would give Peter details of what the Council was up to and Peter, who was currently Deacon of the Mason Trade, would keep John abreast of the building work going on in the town.

The two men walked down the High Street in the direction of the Old Steeple occasioning stares, laughter and sometimes rude shouts from the urchins who always seemed to be around no matter how late it was. The cause of this hilarity was the difference in the two friend's appearance. John Small was a tall man, well over six feet in height with red hair and a red beard. To make matters worse he usually wore a tall hat. Peter David, on the other hand, was five and a half feet and always wore a low crowned wide brimmed hat and an Ulster reaching nearly to his feet giving him the appearance, in silhouette, of a wide-stemmed mushroom. Independently they were quite distinctive; together they looked rather bizarre.

They were heading for Fanny Guthrie's public house in the Overgate. As luck had it that evening they did not take the direct route, but were walking slowly along the wide, well lit Nethergate with the intention of turning up Lindsay Street when they were stopped by a shout followed by the noise of a scuffle. This came from the dark recess of Coutties Wynd, a narrow, unlit street which headed down from the Nethergate towards the docks. The two men immediately dived into the darkness of the wynd just in time to see someone running away down towards Dock Street, no doubt disturbed by the sound of their boots on the cobbles. There was just enough light for them to see that two bodies lay on the ground. Peter produced a stump of a candle from his pocket and lit it. They could now see that one was very still but the other one was clearly alive and trying to sit up. Peter got down on his knees and felt the still man's pulse.

"Nothing," he said. "I'm afraid he's deed."

John had taken off his jacket and had placed it under the smaller figure's head, which was bleeding. Both men's eyes were becoming adapted to the dark and they could now see that the man John was helping was in fact a boy and a brown skinned boy at that. The dead man, in contrast was clearly white. Both were well dressed in European clothes.

"This must hae been a robbery gone wrang," said Peter. "They were probably coming up frae the Docks and, being strangers didna have the sense to stick tae the lighted streets. Still, its no aften that thieves murder you in Dundee."

John had noticed that the dead man still had his watch and chain, and was about to say something to the effect that he was not sure it was a robbery, when the boy opened his eyes and tried to sit up.

"Lie still," said John. "We'll get ye taken tae the infirmary. Ye've had a bad knock on the heid. Peter, could you call for help. We'll need the police and a stretcher."

The boy moved his eyes up and down as if encouraging John to look at something. Eventually John realised that he was indicating his pocket in which his hand was deeply thrust. John carefully felt in the pocket and found a small packet tightly clutched in the boy's hand. When he felt John's fingers on the packet he released his grip and nodded slightly encouraging John to remove the object.

The boy raised his head. "Rakhana ….Chupa," he whispered.

"Quick Peter, he's speaking in a foreign language. Come and listen wi' me. Maybe between us we can mak oot what he's saying."

"Say it again boy."

"Rakhana …..chupa." He fell back then raised himself again, "meeree pita …Kampani …nama," then sank into unconsciousness.

"Peter, have ye got that notebook ye aye carry wi' ye in case someone asks for an estimate?"

Peter searched in the large pockets of his Ulster and produced the notebook and a small pencil.

"Lets see if we can get thae words doon just as the boy said them – there'll be someone at the docks who can tell us what they mean."

By this time a small crowd had gathered at the entrance to the wynd and through it burst the imposing figure of Inspector Angus McLeod.

"Fitz a' this then?" said the Inspector and then, on seeing John and Peter, "Oh its you twa! I micht hae kent!"

Peter and John knew Angus McLeod well. For several years before being elected to the Council John had been a Police Commissioner and had got to know all the Inspectors and their staff. Indeed he and Peter had helped Angus solve the "Case of the Missing Narwhal Tusk" a couple of years previously, although the Inspector had conveniently forgotten the extent of the assistance he had received.

"Oh aye Angus," said Peter. "We heard a shout and came to investigate but, as you can see, we were too late for one of them. I think the boy'll be fine if you get him tae the Infirmary quickly. We just caught a glimpse of someone running off."

"Well, its clear cut this time," said Angus. "There's nae mystery here. They twa were coming up frae the docks and got robbed. They must hae fought back and the assailant stabbed this yin and dinged the boy on the heid."

Turning to John who was still supporting the boys head, "Did he say onything?"

"Only a few words in a foreign tongue," said John.

A "cradle" and a couple of wagons had now arrived and Angus took over conveying the body and the boy to the morgue and Infirmary respectively.

"Come on," said John. "We can do nothing mair here. Lets go on to Fanny's. I've something tae show you."

The two friends continued on their interrupted walk oblivious of the tall figure who was cautiously following them. They went into Fanny Guthrie's. It was warm –almost too warm after the cold of the street - and the atmosphere was smoky with a strong smell of whisky and beer. It was still quite early so the pub was not very busy. Once they were installed in a booth at the back, John took the little parcel from his pocket.

"Lets see what this is then," he said.

"I notice ye didna mention it tae Angus," observed Peter.

"Not till we've looked at it. The lad gave it tae me and I'm no turning it over tae yon great lump of a policeman till I know what it is and why the person who was supposedly robbed still had it on him."

By this time John had removed several layers of waterproof wrappings and held in his hand a little soft leather pouch. He carefully opened it and......

"Guidsakes," exclaimed Peter. "Is that real!"

The object that had occasioned the outburst from the normally imperturbable Peter David was a rather large emerald. Even in the dim light of the room they could see it was flawless. John rapidly wrapped it up again before anyone in the public house could see it.

"Yes, I think it is," he said. "I'm just wondering which of the three was the one that was robbed."

"Well surely the young lad wouldn't have given it to you if he had been the thief."

"No, you certainly wouldna think so," said John, slipping the emerald, now safely back in its protective cloth, into his waistcoat pocket. "He was weel dressed. And did you see his hands? He's never done a days work in his life. He certainly isn't aff one o' the jute boats. I think, unlike the slightly naive Inspector McLeod, that there *is* a mystery worth investigating, eh Peter!"

"I expect they will be making a drawing of the deed man – we should try and get a hold of a copy, we could pass it round the toun and see if anyone kens him."

"I wonder if the boy's in danger," said John, almost to himself. "Still I expect he'll be safe in the Infirmary. Ye'd have tae be a brave man tae get past some o' they nurses!"

By this time they had finished their drinks and the pub had begun to fill up.

"You'd best get off noo, Peter, or your Bella will be thinking you've fallen doon one o' the holes they keep digging in the streets. I see the Provost has just turned up to find out what's happened. He thinks the hale toun revolves around him, Nae doubt he'll be complaining about not being sent for. I'll hae to smooth his ruffled feathers and gie him an edited account of our exploits. The wee man's affy verbose so I probably won't get away for at least half an oor."

"Fine John, I'll come round tae the shop aboot ten the morn's morn and we can decide on a strategy. Of course I'm sorry that a man's deid, but it'll be good to try and solve a case again."

And with that Peter left, leaving John to contend with the small crowd which now surrounded the Provost.

Chapter 2

In which we meet Dod properly

Peter David walked quickly for a small man and was soon past the Wellgate and hurrying up the Hilltown. As its name suggests, the Hilltown is a long street which goes straight up a fairly steep hill. Anyone who lived halfway up the Hilltown was likely to be fit. Peter knew this part of Dundee like the back of his hand; his father had bought a tenement there in the early years of the century and Peter had lived there all his life. As he got about half way up he thought he heard footsteps behind him. Changing his pace a little he heard the soft steps also changing pace.

"Aha, ye think ye can creep up on me, my mannie," he thought and kept walking. Peter had two advantages in any encounter with footpads. Firstly there was his famous hat. As a young man he had noticed that, even with the best precautions, masons occasionally dropped things – hammers, chisels, stone, brick – and having no intention of being brained, he had had constructed a hat lined with steel and well at the edge of the next entry.

"That's your game, is it – one to jump in front of me and one to take me from behind".

Then everything happened at once. The shadow turned into a young man brandishing a stick. Peter dropped on one knee and with a sweeping motion caught his assailant on the leg just at the knee joint. The crack was nearly as loud as the cry of pain as the youth went down. There was a dull metallic clunk as the second assailant swung his cudgel at Peter' head. The hat, however, deflected the blow and Peter padded. This had been tested several times during his career – it could take a dropped hammer at twenty feet – it could certainly take a cudgel. His second advantage was more aggressive than defensive. Many years ago he had had the core of his walking stick bored out and filled with lead. He could break bones with even the narrow end.

Just as he was about to turn and face his follower, he noticed a slight shadow turned and cracked his stick down on to the attacker, hitting him hard on the shoulder.

"Right ye glaikit wee nyaffs, who did ye think ye were dealing wi'?"

"I dinna ken," said the younger one, clutching his bruised knee. " Ah wiz jist gi'en a shilling to jump oot and fleg you"

"No, I can see you're no the brains behind this. Get yersel' aff. If I see you around here again it won't be your leg that'll be hurting"

"Now, you," Peter said, addressing the older man while leaning on his lead weighted stick. "Speak."

"Ah was approached by a man just as me and the boy was goin' intae Fanny's. He gave me half a guinea to knock ye doon and search yer pooches. He said ah could keep onything I foond except a wee packet."

"What was in the packet?"

"He didna tell me. Just said that when I brocht it tae him he wad gie me another half guinea. Ah'm a puir man, sir, a guinea is an affy lot o' money. I wouldnae hae hurt ye, sir, honest."

"What did he look like." Peter pulled himself up to his full five and a half feet and held the stick in front of him with both hands.

"He was English. He was affy weel dressed wi' checked troosers, a low hat and nae beard but fair side-whiskers and a big gold watch chain – oh and he had a wee pistol inside his coat."

"Right then you. If I see you in Dundee again ye'll be up afore the Baillies for attempted murder."

At that Mr David turned on his heel and strode off. As he approached his close he heard a little voice hailing him.

"Maister Davie, are you a' richt?"

"Is that you Dod? Aye I'm fine – a lot better thae they twa idiots - but its lucky you're here - I need a message delivered quickly."

"Nae bother Maister Davie."

"Ye ken whar Baillie Small the baker lives – the corner o' the Hawkhill and Hunter Street. Go tae him as quickly as you can. Try the bakehoose first – he's maist likely tae be there. Tell him what happened here and warn him that the man who sent these gowks to knock me doon is efter him as weel and that he has a pistol – oh and tell him the man's after the packet."

And Dod Johnston (eleven years old) was off through the closes and pends by the shortest rout possible to the Hawkhill, followed closely by a yellowish shadow.

It was a good half hour before John had disentangled himself from the Provost and was able to walk back towards the West Port and home. He decided to go straight into the bake house to check that everything was set for the morning's baking. He had a good assistant and two apprentices - but the name over the shop door was John Allan Small and it was important to make sure that the quality of his bread and cakes was always good. He had just checked that the fire in the oven was properly laid when the heard a movement at the open door. Turning round he saw a gentleman slowly advancing into the light of the room. The man took something out of an inside pocket of his coat. John saw it was a pistol.

"Your friend will have been knocked down and searched by now as a precaution – I hired a couple of ruffians to do that. But I think *you* must have my property - and I want it now."

John did not move.

"I won't be threatened in my own shop," he said. "If you've lost something, go to the police."

"Don't mess with me," whispered the intruder. "I killed one man tonight, and he was not the first. I won't worry about adding a baker to my tally. Quick – hand it over!"

He was stooping slightly to cock the pistol, keeping his eyes locked on John's all the time, when he suddenly let out a scream, dropped the pistol and clutched his right buttock. Instantly John moved forward and punched him on the jaw knocking him to the floor and revealing a slightly worried looking small boy and a less worried looking dog.

"Guidsakes, man, wha are you? I think you've saved my life."

"I'm ca'ed Dod Johnston, Maister Sma'. Maister Davie sent me tae warn you that ye might be attacked, but I didna get here in time."

"It's a good job ye got here when ye did," said John. "What did ye dae tae him," he continued, pointing at the man on the floor.

"Ah aye cairry a sharp pencil in ma pooch, Maister Sma'. Ah thoucht sticking it in his bum it micht be enough tae …..whit's the word … distract, aye, distract him."

"It certainly did that," replied John, and a good thing for me it did. He continued, "Is Peter a' richt?"

"O aye. He whacked the lads sent tae waylay him wi' his lead stick. They telt him they were tae get a wee packet aff him."

John picked up the pistol and carefully hid it behind some tins of shortbread.

"Quick, Dod, search his pockets."

"There's a wee pooch o' sovereigns, Maister Sma'!"

"Aye weel. we'll take these till the police arrive. I've still got the whistle Sergeant Sharp gave me a couple of years ago."

John nipped outside and gave three sharp blasts, then came back in and studied the man lying on the floor. His hat had been knocked off and showed that he had blond hair and a pair of pale side-whiskers. Checked trousers, expensive boots and a long coat completed the outfit. Round his waist was a large gold watch-chain,

"I'll see if I've a bit of rope in the back," said John, but as he turned the gentleman sprung up from the floor and darted out the door, knocking over constable Black as he escaped.

"Oh damn, we've lost him."

"Aye but we've got his money – and he'll no be sittin' doon fur a day or twa! I expect he's the same man that peyd the twa lads tae knock doon Maister Davie," piped up Dod.

"Did ye hear him speak?" said the constable.

"Aye," said John. "He was English I think."

"He spoke affy guid English," said Dod. "He didna sound like the English sailors ye hear roond the docks ….."

Dod broke off suddenly realising that he was speaking to a policeman and a Baillie.

"Good lad. I think you're right," said John - turning to constable Black. "This young man probably saved my life," and then described the incident of the "pistol and the pencil" as it would become known in the coffee houses and pubs of Dundee.

"I'll hae to dae something for you, but for the now, here's a florin, its a' the change I've got and here's a poke – fill it with any cookies or cakes ye can find. Tell Mr David what happened here and remind him that I'm expecting him at ten the morn's morn."

Yesterday's cookies they may have been, but Dod was lucky if he ever ate a three day old cookie or cake, so he crammed the bag full and with a "Guid nicht, Maister Sma'.", he vanished into the night.

Chapter 3

In which Dod considers his future and thinks about his past

It had been a long and eventful evening. It began with the excitement of seeing the Deacon clouting the twa ruffians. Then being asked to take an important message to Baillie Sma' "as fast as ye can rin". And when he got there seeing yon man pointing a pistol at the Baillie. He still didn't know what made him stick his wee pencil in the man's bum – but he now knew it was the right thing to have done and it had probably changed his life for ever. "Maister Sma' said he would hae to dae something for me" he muttered to himself as he walked back from Peter David's house, where he had told his story or been "debriefed" (as the Deacon had ca'ed it). Even Mistress Davie had seemed pleased – she wasn't always pleased when the Deacon slipped Dod or his friends a penny - and ca'ed him a "wee hero" and made him eat a plate of soup.

He walked a few hundred yards up the hill and then dived into a long dark pend that took him eventually to the ramshackle tenement where he and his mother rented a single room on the second floor. It was a short distance in space and time, but a world of difference in comfort from the Deacon's house. At least it wasn't on the ground floor which was damp and prone to visits by rats, or on the top floor which leaked whenever it rained, but it *was* one small room with a single window, no running water and, of course, no lavatory, which was out the back, next to the midden and shared by the sixty or so inhabitants of the tenement.

His mother was, as expected, asleep, the smell of whisky indicating that she had just been paid, and more importantly, that she would probably not be at work tomorrow. "Ah well." thought Dod "at least I've got twa shillin's and a poke of breid and cakes." This sent him thinking about the idea of "daein' something" for him once again. He would have to make sure that the "something" was what he wanted and not what they thought would be good for him. They might be thinking of getting him an apprenticeship, but he was sure he did not want to be a mason – he didn't fancy working on the scaffolds, there were too many accidents and the stone dust made you cough – and he was not sure about rising at three or four in the morning to be a baker. What he really wanted was to go to school and learn things. He could read – he had taught himself with the help of old newspapers – and he could write a bit and count and knew a little about the world outside Dundee from his frequent visits to the docks.

"It's an awfu' thing this future!", he thought as he crammed an angel cake into his mouth, with the self justification that the cream ones would not keep, "It mak's you think about the past as weel." What did he know about himself? He was called Dod (that's Scotch for George) Johnston, his mithers name was Jeannie Brown and she hadn't married his faither, who was called Thomas. He was eleven and a bit years old. When he had asked his mother a year or two ago when his birthday was she replied "Hoo can I mind. Ah was too busy screamin' wi' pain tae look at the calendar." And then followed up with "Mind, they telt me it was near the day of the Queen's coronation so you bein' the clever one can find it oot for yoursel'." Which he did. So Dod considered his birthday – his official birthday – he liked to think of it, to be the 28th June 1838.

Over several years Dod had extracted his and his mother's story from her. It was far from unusual. Her father was a ploughman employed on one of the big farms in the parish of Kinfauns at the far end of the Carse of Gowrie. When she was seventeen she fell in love with the farmer's eighteen year old son Thomas. When she became pregnant Thomas, who was also in love, promised to marry her. His father, George Johnston, had other ideas. Thomas was packed off to an uncle near Glasgow "to learn modern farming methods" and Jeannie, once young Dod was weaned, was sent off to Dundee, where it was believed (or at least hoped) she had relatives. She got some satisfaction by insisting on calling her boy after his grandfather but it did neither her nor Dod much good. Dod was left with his grandmother (his mother's mother that is) till he was five years old, when he too was sent away to join his mother. "A boy should be with his mother," said the Minister, although everyone knew that the real reason was to avoid paying for Dod's schooling, and he was taken on the Perth to Dundee coach by the Session Clerk, who had business to conduct in town. There the little boy was delivered to Jeannie, who had never had the time or the opportunity to learn the skills of motherhood.

So for the past six years Dod had lived with his mother, who had been abandoned by her relatives (if they ever existed) in a series of single rooms of variable quality, depending on whether Jeannie was in work or not. Even the best of these was so dire, however, that Dod spent a lot of time on the street. They never moved far from the same district, though, so Dod came to know the Hilltown nearly as well as the Deacon. In a country Parish they would have made him go to school; here in the town, no-one cared and so, since school cost money, he had to educate himself. When he was eight his mother had started him at the spinning mill where she worked. The work was long and hard, sometimes eighteen hours a day, and many of the boys fell asleep at the looms which usually resulted in a beating from the overseer. Mill fever, a debilitating illness caused by breathing the dust in the mill, was endemic, and accidents were common. Many boys lost fingers or worse when exhausted. About a year after he started his best friend caught his neck-cloth in a spinning bobbin and was choked to death. On that day Dod left the factory and never returned. Although small he was both quick and personable and soon began to make some sort of living running messages for people. He didn't make quite as much as at the mill, and sometimes he was forced to steal food to eat, but it was a much healthier life. It gave him the opportunity to talk to anyone who could spend the time and thus he acquired an education of sorts. He had taught himself to read by spelling out the words of old newspapers and magazines. Sometimes a bookseller would put pages from one of Mr Dickens latest offerings in his window to whet his customers' appetites and Dod read them with excitement. Earlier his year he had managed to read the beginning of *David Copperfield.* He was particularly fond of the docks and spent hours talking with and listening to the sailors.

On the same day he walked out of the mill for the last time, he met his shadow. He was wandering along the bank of one of the cooling ponds near Dens Road throwing stones in the water when he saw a small orangy-brown hairy object. Further inspection showed it was alive and detailed investigation revealed that it was a half drowned puppy. Dod wrapped it in his jacket and took it home. She acquired her name, Shadow, from the fact that from that day onwards she never left Dod's side. His mother was not happy about another mouth to feed – "Yer no' keeping yon mangy bit of skin and bane!" - but as usual Dod got his own way and

Shadow had shared his bed and his life from that day on. She was not a big dog, but she was brave – her mother was probably an Irish terrier and her father a street mongrel – and had saved Dod from a beating by older boys on more than one occasion. Most dogs consider their master to be the pack leader, but Shadow was even more devoted to Dod than normal – he was the first thing she saw after awakening from the trauma of being nearly drowned – and she never voluntarily left his side, although she rapidly learnt to keep out of sight if required.

Did Dod feel he was hard done by? He certainly would never have had that thought. Life was what it was. Life was better in Dundee than it had been in the country. If he had still been living on the farm he would be working in the fields by now instead of mooching round the docks and pinching a chop or a couple of sausages from Mr Niven's shop in the Wellgate (although ye had to mak share it was young Mr Niven who was in the shop – no-one risked stealing from old Mr Niven. He'd once gone tae the jail for near killing someone for stealing from his shop). Did he miss not having a father? Lots of boys had no fathers and some with fathers wished they hadn't when they came in drunk and beat them. His father would be married by this time; maybe Dod had wee brothers and sisters, but unless things changed a lot he would never get to meet them. He only wished his mother would not drink so much. He loved her – how could he not – but she had never got over being forced to leave her home and the boy she loved. Life as a factory worker was hard and she was often miserable and sharp with Dod. Which thoughts brought him back to the present and what he should say to Mr Small tomorrow – because he was certainly going to keep up the acquaintance. Maybe he could go to sea – on a whaler to the Arctic, or to the Indies, or to America ...... And so he fell asleep.

Chapter 4

In which Dod is given a task and Mr Small investigates

The next morning at exactly ten o'clock Peter David entered Mr Small's baker's shop at the corner of the Hawkhill and Hunter Street.

"Good morning, John, I tak' it you're nane the worse for your experience last night."

"No. Peter, I'm fine – although if your young lad Dod hadna been there things micht have been very different. I think yon man would hae killed me withoot a second thought. How about you, Peter, I hear thae miscreants won't be showing their faces in the Hilltown for a while"

"Amateurs, John, mere amateurs. I mind the time before gaslight when you really had to be careful going home at night. I may be getting on, but my ears and eyes are still working. Talking of which, there's a wee pair of ears and eyes lurking ootside the shop. He followed me from my hoose – doesn't think I know he's there. I was thinking – if we are to continue with this investigation, young Dod might be useful to us. He could go to places and hear things that we couldn't – *and* he saw the man that took the pistol to you, and could recognise him."

"That's what worries me. Peter, if yon fellow has committed murder once, or more, he'd have no scruples about a wee boy who could identify him. But still, you're right, Dod is in this whether he likes it or not - and I imagine he does like! Better to keep him close than risk him "investigating" on his own."

"Wullie!" This to one of his apprentices. "See that young man standing in the close across the road - the one wi' the dug, who's trying no' tae be seen. Tak him into the bakehoose and gie him a scone. Tell him the Deacon and I will be in in a minute."

Peter finished his pipe and John gave instructions to the other apprentice, who was minding the shop, then they went through the back of the shop into the bake house, where Dod was stuffing himself with a new-baked scone.

"Back at the scene of your crime," joked Peter. "Its nae often that a lad gets praise for sticking a sherp pencil in a man's backside!"

"Now here's the thing, Dod," said John. "I would rather keep you oot o' this, but I don't think you'd let me.

And anyway you could be a lot of use just listening to the gossip around the toun. You and I are the only ones who know what the man who attacked me looks like. Fortunately I don't think he got a look at you."

"No," mumbled Dod through a mouthful of scone. "I dinna think he saw me. I kept weel back oot of the light while he was on the flair."

"Weel, if you are tae be involved you'd better know the background." And John described what happened last night in Coutties Wynd, ending up by giving him a copy of the words he had written out.

He finished with, "I can't show you what was in the packet yet, because its weel hidden, but ye'll get tae see it later."

"But just mind, Dod," said Peter. "This is no a game. The man's dangerous. He's probably killed more than once and so he's nothing to lose by killing again. Now to try and preserve your anonymity – there's a braw big word Dod – ye mustn't be seen with either the Baillie or me any more than necessary. Come to the hoose here, or to my hoose when you need to speak to us. And – and this is very important – Inspector McLeod mustna know you are involved or he'll stop it dead – he might even lock you up to keep you safe. It'll be difficult enough for Mr Small and me to get involved with the investigation. The Inspector might just have the sense tae realise that there's mair too it now than a simple robbery but I'm shair he doesna want help, and if we hadn't been attacked we would hae found it difficult to persuade him."

"Right," said Dod, his mouth now empty. "Whit can I dae tae help?"

"The first thing you can do is to gae upstairs and see Mistress Small. She's affy keen to see you. I think she wants to thank you for saving her husband's life. Now I have tae warn you her thanks will involve food – but it might also involve washing – she's gae keen on washing – and probably some of our Alec's old claes.

Dod interrupted him with a hurt expression on his face.

"Ah dinna mind a bit o' washing Mr Sma'. Ah gae tae the Public Baths every couple o' weeks if ah can afford it!"

"Oh, aye, sorry," said John. "Anyway after she's finished with you I've a wee job you can do. Tak that paper with the words that the boy said tae me – gae doon tae the docks and see if any of the sailors recognise the language and can tell ye what they mean. If ye find such a man ye can tell him that there's money in it for him if he keeps his mooth shut aboot it."

And Dod was sent upstairs to see the redoubtable Elizabeth Small.

Meanwhile the two men had put on their coats and hats, picked up their walking sticks and had begun to walk down the Hawkhill in the direction of the police station in Bell Street. The Hawkhill was a busy street, lined with shops. The two men had to negotiate themselves between unloading carts, message boys carrying heavy parcels and women with laden shopping baskets. This was John's territory – he was their councillor, had been in charge of the police, and supplied a goodly number with their bread – and was immediately recognisable because of his height and red beard. He stopped to shake hands or raise his hat from time to time, occasionally asking about the health of someone's mother or child – not because he needed their votes; there were only a few hundred voters in the Ward – all property owners, but because he was just that kind of man. Peter, of course, knew far fewer people in this part of town, but, as they progressed eastwards, there was more building work, and he began to recognise a few masons, often high on scaffolding, and raised his famous steel hat.

Soon they arrived at the police station in Bell Street where they were met by a none too pleased Inspector McLeod.

"Baillie Small, Deacon David, this is a surprise."

"It shouldna be," said Peter, "after the events of last night. Did you think that we would stay out of this when we've been attacked and, in the Baillie's case, near murdered?"

"We willna interfere with your investigation, Angus", said John. "But we hae a lot o' contacts between us and we have helped in the past …."

"Have you any more information about the deed man and the boy?" asked Peter.

"Aye," said Inspector McLeod. "They arrived aboot a week ago and took lodgings just aff the High Street, I was just on my way tae interview the landlady. I suppose you twa want tae come tae."

Clearly they did and so the three of them walked slowly along Ward Street, along the north side of the Old

Burial ground and down Reform Street before reaching the High Street. There Inspector McLeod led them into Campbell's Close where they found Mrs Ogilvie's Lodging House (single gentlemen a speciality). Mrs Ogilvie was a largish lady who was never seen without her hat, even in her own house. She stood at the top of the stairs leading up to her front door.

"Guid morning," said the Inspector. "I'm Inspector McLeod and these gentlemen are assisting me in this case. Baillie Small and Mr Peter David."

"Aye, I recognise you Baillie. My sister lives at the end of the Overgate, near the West Port and swears by your breid. Come in gentlemen. I expect you'll want tae see the rooms that the poor gentleman and the wee boy occupied."

"Do we know who they are?" asked Peter.

"The man used the name 'Jasper Diprose' when he arrived," said Mrs Ogilvie. "The two of them turned up ten days ago. They insisted on separate bedrooms and paid two weeks rent in advance. The boy was just called Bali. I assumed at first that he was a servant, but he didna behave much like one."

As Mrs Ogilvie was speaking she led them up the central stairs to the second floor where the two visitors had rented a sitting room and two bedrooms. A young lad was standing in the middle of the room.

"This is my nephew Harry – or as he likes tae cry himself noo – Henry - Ogilvie. He had much mair tae do wi' the pair than I did."

"Angus, why don't you go back doonstairs wi' Mrs Ogilvie and tak her statement," said John. "I'll just hae a quick look aroond up here, although there doesn't seem tae be much tae see."

Speaking quietly to Peter he said, "Could you go doonstairs with them and pretend tae be interested in Mrs Ogilvie. I think I'll get mair out of the boy if she's no' aroond.

Henry, now free from the presence of his aunt, was keen to talk and proved to be much more useful. He was clearly upset about the death of his employer.

"Mr Diprose said to my aunt that he needed a man-servant for while he was in Dundee, because he could not bring his usual servant with him. Young Bali was definitely no servant – in fact sometimes he seemed to be in charge.

They'd plenty of money and when he sent me out to buy stuff he sometimes said – I'll try to get this right - that "John Cupny would pey for it"; but he had an affy English accent and sometimes I coulna be sure of his words. The first thing I had tae dae – to do - was to go and buy a complete outfit for Bali - he was about my size. Then – and this might be important – he had me down at the docks every day to see if any jute boats came in. If one did, and there were three last week, he and Bali would go down to look at them. I think they were looking for someone in particular."

"And," continued Henry," that's what happened yesterday. I came back about two o' clock to tell them that a jute boat had been sighted. They rushed out – and never came back…."

"Thanks, Henry, you've been very helpful. Ye might like tae know that Bali will likely be all right. I'm going up to the Infirmary this afternoon to see how he is. If you want to know when he can have visitors, or you can think of anything else that might help, you can find me at my shop on the corner of Hawkhill and Hunter Street."

John paused and turned as he started to go down the stairs. He searched in his pocket.

"Here's a half crown tae yourself – dinna tell your aunt now."

John rejoined Peter and Angus in Mrs Ogilvie's kitchen.

"Angus", he said. "Ye ken my Alec is at the Seminaries and is affy guid at drawing. Could I borrow the drawing of Mr Diprose to let him copy it. Before you say no – I'll get him tae mak' an extra copy for you – that'll save you a bit of money!"

"This is very irregular, John," said Inspector McLeod. "But seeing its you – and we will need another copy and yon artist fellow charges quite a lot – ye can tell your Alec that if he goes tae the police station this efternane he can copy it there."

The three men left the house. Inspector McLeod made his way back to Bell Street on his own. Peter and John let him get out of earshot.

"Something yon Henry said is working away in my mind," said John. "I'm not sure what it is yet, but it'll come tae me. I'd better get back tae the shop. Mind you, I'm still worried that Bali might be in danger. Could you look in at the Infirmary, Peter – I was going tae go mysel' but it's easier for you because it's on your way hame. See how the boy is and tell the Matron, she's ca'ed Mrs Mitchell, that he's tae hae no visitors except you me and, I suppose, Angus, unless I explicitly authorise it. I'm thinking I might send Dod up tae speak tae the boy when he's conscious – it might be less intimidating than you or me."

The two men separated and made their ways home.

Chapter 5

In which Betsey comes to the rescue

John Small owned the whole tenement block at the corner of Hawkhill and Hunter Street. The shop (opening onto the Hawkhill) and the connecting bake-house (opening onto Hunter Street) occupied the ground floor. The second and third floors were let to a variety of tenants, some of whom were family. But the whole of the first floor, which would normally have been two separate flats was connected together by an internal door, which joined the two hallways, and was occupied by John and his extended family. This currently consisted of his wife Elizabeth, their children - Alec who was twelve, a year older than Dod, Betsey who was eleven, George, six and Thomas, five – two apprentices, a servant and John's mother-in-law.

Mistress Small was starting to prepare the midday dinner in the scullery at the back of the kitchen. She had just sent Dod off on his errand with a decent breakfast and a slightly cleaner face and neck. She had got no further than that, but she had let him know that if he turned up on Bath

Night he could join the children. Dod had also been kitted out with a pair of trousers and a jacket which belonged to the Smalls eldest son, Alec. The new clothes, and the clean face, made it unlikely that the mysterious foreigner would recognise Dod even if he had got a look at him. Alec, George and Thomas were at school, but Betsey, who was suffering from a bad cold was in bed. She had got up to meet Dod, who she saw as a bit of a hero, but had been sent back with a hot drink and a book.

The events of last night had started a train of thought in Elizabeth's mind. She had nearly lost John – it didn't bear thinking what would have happened if yon wee boy hadn't been there. She was pregnant, and their last child had died shortly after it was born, so she was already in a highly charged emotional state. This led to her thinking about John's first wife, Isabella, who had died in childbirth. She was always there as a faint presence in Elizabeth's mind - partly because everything they owned, the tenement and the business, had been bought with Isabella's money – and partly because – well – the perfect memory would always be preserved. Whenever she got angry with John she wondered if she was being compared to someone she could never compete with. She had just managed to put the thoughts to the back of her mind and was concentrating on peeling potatoes in a bowl on the kitchen table, when she heard the sound of the front door opening.

"Who's there?" she shouted.

"You do not need to know my name, you only need to do as I say".

This was spoken in upper class English by a tall blond man holding a strange looking knife in front of him.

"Your husband has something of mine – a small packet – give it to me and you will not be hurt."

Elizabeth was not an unusually brave woman, but she was incensed at the thought of someone barging in and threatening her in her own home.

"Get out, you scoundrel," she shouted. "Is it no' enough to try and murder my husband withoot coming into my house and waving yon bit knife about."

The man laughed and took a step forward.

"This can be easy or difficult," he said very softly. and began to advance slowly into the kitchen.

Elizabeth was now behind the kitchen table which was between her and the intruder. She rapidly looked round for something to defend herself with, but there was nothing of much use within reach.

Suddenly the man gave a scream, dropped the knife and clutched his buttocks. Elizabeth saw Betsey standing behind him holding a toasting fork. She had crept out of her bedroom when she heard the shouting and seen the back of the strange man.

"It must be the same man," she thought, "and so his bum must still be sair. Which cheek did Dod say he stabbed – the right I think. If I can jab it in the same place...."

Which is exactly what she did, opening the wound at her second attempt.

Elizabeth threw the basin of water and potato peelings over him, picked up a heavy frying pan, ran round the table and hit him on the shoulder while shouting at the top of her voice, "Betsey, get ootside and shout for help."

Betsey, still I her nightdress, ran out of the front door, down the stairs and into the street. She dashed round the corner into the Hawkhill shouting "Murder, police! There's a man attacking ma mither in the hoose!"

Two carters were unloading barrels at the pub across the road.

"That's Baillie Sma's wee girl, Sandy. Come on."

And Jimmy and Sandy ran round the corner and up the close at 28 Hunter Street just in time to see the intruder staggering out of the door.

"Get a hud of him Jimmy," said Sandy, but Jimmy suddenly cried out and sank to his knees with a nasty stab wound in his arm.

The man slashed at Sandy but fortunately missed and rushed down the stairs and out into the street. Instead of turning into the Hawkhill he ran up Hunter Street, through a close and vanished.

Back in the house Elizabeth was sitting down cradling Betsey in her lap.

"My brave girl", she said. "You saved me."

"It was yon Dod, mither. I was so jealous of him saving faither that I just had to dae something too. I thought that if I could just get the right place, it would be affy sair!"

They were interrupted by Jimmy staggering into the room supported by Sandy.

"He got away, Mistress Sma' and he's hurt Jimmy, here, sair."

Elizabeth roused herself.

"Betsey, get dressed and go down to the shop. Tell Wullie to go and get a doctor, quick. Meanwhile I'll try and stop the bleeding."

the crossing thing

The first thing John Small noticed as he approached Hunter Street was an unattended cart, with half its beer barrels unloaded. A small boy was clutching the reigns of the horses and trying to stop them wandering off.

"They're up at your hoose, Maister Sma'," he shouted. "I think there's been a murder."

John dashed up the stairs, hardly daring to think what might have happened. The first thing he saw was Elizabeth and Betsey, very much alive, fussing round a strange man who was bleeding and being attended by the Smalls' doctor.

"This is Jimmy and Sandy," piped up Betsey. "They were delivering beer across the road and came up to help us. Jimmy been sair hurt."

Eventually the whole story came out and the doctor announced that Jimmy's wound was not serious but he would be off work for a few weeks.

"First things first," said John. "I have to thank you twa for coming to help. You'll no be out of pocket, Jimmy, I'll see your boss and pey your wages till you can work again."

When the two carters ⟨the people⟩ had left John sat down at the kitchen table with Elizabeth and Betsey.

"This is all my fault," said John. "I kent the man was dangerous – he's killed one man that we know of and attacked Peter and me – I should have telt you to lock the door and let naebody in you didn't ken. The boys can't go back to school this afternoon, They'll hae to stay at home till we catch the murderer."

As if on cue, Alec, George and Thomas came back from school for their dinner and the events of the morning had to be recounted again.

"That's no' fair," said Alec. "First Dod, and now Betsey gets to be heroes and I have to go to school and miss a'thing!"

"Don't worry, Alec," said John. "I've a very important job for you, "I need copies of the sketch of the murdered man that the police artist made. Angus said you could copy it if you went tae the police station this afternoon. I'll take you there, leave you for an hour or two and collect you later. You're no' to come back on your ain as long as the murderer's loose. I want three copies – one I promised to give to Inspector McLeod, one to show aboot the toun and one I want to send somewhere. No. I'm no' telling you any more, but something that the man's manservant, Henry, said gave me an idea. If I'm right I'll explain everything."

Alec was an accomplished artist and was somewhat mollified by being given an important task he knew he could do well.

"Maybe Alec could make a drawing of the funny knife if mother and me made rough sketches," said Betsey. "It was triangular, wi' a funny handle."

The three of them got out paper and pencil and in a quarter of an hour Alec had produced a drawing that both Betsey and Elizabeth agreed looked very much like the strange knife or dagger. It was about a foot long, triangular in shape, with a strange looking hilt which seemed to go up the sides of the wrist.

"I've seen a picture of that knife, I'm sure," said John, "but I canna remember where. Let me give the drawing to Peter. His son Willie goes to the Watt Institute. Maybe he can find it in one of the books in the library."

Chapter 6

In which Dod goes down to the Docks and meets
Captain Melville

Dod was a relatively happy boy if you excepted his permanent worry about his mother's health and state of mind. But today he was exceptionally happy. He had just eaten the best breakfast he could remember, he was impressed with his new clothes which were more fashionable, much more intact and much much cleaner than his old ones – and, to be fair, having a bit of a wash was a bonus. It would save him going to the Public Baths this week. He had also quite taken to Betsey, who had got out of bed to meet him and seemed to think he was very brave. Like most children in his circumstances he was both fascinated by and attracted to proper families. He was daydreaming about being adopted by the Smalls when he remembered his mother and immediately felt guilty. Anyway he had a job to do – an important job. He was determined to find someone who understood the words Mr Small had copied down if he had to ask every sailor at the docks.

By this time he had got to the end of the Overgate, had turned down School Wynd and had stopped to read the paper again in the shadow of St Mary's tower. He looked carefully and tried to read the words which Mr Small had copied out – "Rakhana …..chupa.' 'meeree pita ….. Kampani ……lnama" – but they were very strange. "Oh well", he thought, "someone will ken what they mean, There's every nation in the warld at the Dundee docks." He turned left up the Nethergate, pushing himself through the crowds and avoiding the ever present danger of iron shod cart wheels. He knew a few boys who had been crippled or even killed by a cart suddenly going backwards or moving too fast. Soon he turned down Crichton Street and emerged into the Greenmarket.

Under any other circumstance he would have spent some time wandering round the stalls, looking on the ground for spoilt fruit or vegetables, or even pocketing the odd apple when a stallholder was not looking. But today he was a boy on a mission and he ran quickly through the market and on to the quay of the Earl Grey Dock. Dod loved the docks and came down as often as he could. Since it was winter the whalers were in port and the smell of boiling blubber hung in the air. The quay was busy as usual – ships were loading and unloading. The Earl Grey was mainly occupied by fishing boats and   smaller ships that did the coastal or continental routes, bringing flax and timber from the Baltic, wine from France, oranges from Spain and the more prosaic, but equally necessary coal and iron from Fife and the Lothians and, more recently, from Newcastle. The larger ocean going vessels tended to use the William IV dock next door. There were usually one or two jute ships from India – there were more and more of these every year - and grain ships from America. As well as the people who were working there were the inevitable onlookers, including sailors whose ships were in port or those looking for a berth. If you listened carefully you could hear most of the languages of the western world and not a few from the Indies. He looked around to see if there was anyone he knew and finally noticed an old sailor who had taken a liking to him and who he often sat down to talk – or more likely listen – to.

"Guid morning, Calum," he shouted, as he pushed his way over to where Calum McDonald was sitting on a bollard smoking an evil smelling clay pipe.

"And a guid morning to you tae, young Dod What brings you doon tae the docks today? And what's the great hurry?"

"I've got an affy important job to dae," said Dod. "Baillie Sma' has asked me tae find out what thae foreign words mean.", and he thrust the paper under Calum's nose.

"Wait a meenit. There's nae use showing me that," said the sailor. "Ye ken weel I canna read. Noo calm doon and tell me the hale story."

So Dod briefly recounted the events of yesterday.

"Weel," said Calum. "That's quite a story. Lets try yir wards. If you sound them oot tae me I might at least recognise the language."

So Dod carefully spoke the words as well as he was able.

"Rakhana …..chupa.' 'meeree pita ….. Kampani ……lnama"

"Weel," said Calum. "They're no French or Spanish. They're no German or Dutch. Dinna worry, Dod, I ken just the man tae ask. We'll have tae go along the quay to the William IV, the Captain likes tae moor there."

So Dod and Calum threaded their way though the crowds of people along the quay, under the Victoria arch and down to the bottom right-hand corner of the William IV dock where the *Oxalis* was moored.

"Anybody on board?", shouted Calum.

"Aye, there's me, "said a young sailor, sticking his head out of the hold.

"Is the Captain on board?"

"Aye, he's in his cabin."

"Could ye ask him if ald Calum can come aboard tae hae a word wi' him?"

The sailor emerged from the hold, walked across the deck, knocked at the cabin door and went in. He returned a second or two later.

"Aye Captain Melville says tae come aboard."

Calum and Dod climbed up the gangplank, across the deck and knocked at the door of the Captain's cabin. For once Shadow was told not to follow Dod, but to stay on the quay.

"Come in Calum," came a voice from inside.

They went into the small cabin. Captain Melville rose as they entered,

"Ah, Calum, you've brought a visitor," and with a sweeping bow, "James Whitton Melville, master of the *Oxalis,* at your service. You're a bit young to be seeking a berth I'd say!"

Dod was normally a loquacious boy, often considered to be a bit precocious, but in the presence of the Captain he was tongue-tied. Captain Melville was indeed enough to cause most boys to look twice. He was not exactly dressed as a pirate, but he certainly did not look like an ordinary sailor. He grew his hair a little longer than was fashionable and sported a small moustache instead of the customary beard. He was dressed in his "shore clothes" – a pale blue coat, worn over a fancy waistcoat and tight white trousers with knee boots. He was also very young for a Captain. Indeed he was one of the youngest Captains operating from Dundee.

Calum took over.

"This is Dod Johnston, Captain Melville. He's been sent by Baillie Sma' to find oot what some wards mean. They sound to me like the sort of words the lascars use."

"Oh you're the boy the whole town is talking about," said the Captain – "Well maybe not the whole town, but everyone who frequents the Exchange Coffee House." and he explained to a somewhat bemused Dod that a number of the more prominent townsmen were inclined to meet in the morning to take a dish of coffee and, more importantly, to exchange gossip. Peter David was one of the number – he had gone to the coffee house before meeting Mr Small – and all the talk that morning had been of the murder in Coutties Wynd and the assaults on Peter and John - accounts which may have been slightly exaggerated in the telling. The image of the six and a half foot tall Baillie being saved by wee ragged eleven year old boy had seemed particularly amusing to many of the men present.

"We had better not keep the Baillie waiting then, let me see the words. You're right Calum. They're not European. They might be Hindustani or one of the other languages spoken on the jute boats. Leave this with me and I'll ask around."

Dod's attention suddenly wavered as he noticed a movement at the top of the cabinet behind the Captain's table. This focussed into a furry bundle showing a fine set of teeth.

"Whit's that?" cried Dod.

"Ah, you've made the acquaintance of Rodriguez. Come down, Rodriguez and meet Mr George Johnston – I think I'll call you George – much more fitting for a hero!"

The monkey jumped down onto the table and proffered a small paw to Dod who very tentatively put his hand out.

"Does he bite?"

"Only if he doesn't like you!" said the Captain. "Go on - shake his hand."

Dod stretched forwards and the monkey took his index finger in its little fingers and solemnly shook it.

"See, he likes you," said the Captain. "He's useful in a fight, you know. He once bit the ear off someone who was trying to hit me with a belaying pin!"

The monkey retreated back to his vantage point on the top of the cupboard and yawned, showing his useful teeth.

"Whit does he eat?" said Dod.

"Fruit and vegetables," said the Captain. "Usually its apples and pears, but he loves oranges and grapes. When we do a French run I always try and get him a bunch of grapes."

Captain Melville stood up.

"Tell Baillie Small that I will come round to his house about five o'clock this evening and let him know what I've found out. You can also tell Mistress Small that I expect to be able to sample some of her excellent cakes," he said with a broad grin.

Calum and Dod went down the gangplank and onto the quay, where Shadow was waiting.

"He's........ I've never met onyone like him. And yon monkey........"

"Oh aye, Captain Melville is a braw man. He's one of the youngest Masters sailing from Dundee. And for a' he dresses like a gentleman he's a fine sailor – he's been at sea since he was a lad o' fourteen."

"Hoo old is he noo," said Dod.

"I think he's aboot thirty year ald," said Calum.

And Dod walked back up the Greenmarket muttering under his breath "The same age of my ain faither."

Chapter 7

In which Dod obtains some oranges.

A fter dinner John went down to the bake-house for a short while to check on the apprentices, then back up to his "study" where he wrote a letter. Then he and Alex left the house, making sure that Elizabeth locked the door behind them. They walked down the Hawkhill to the West Port, then up North Tay Street and along Bell Street to the Police Station. There Alex was left in a the corner of Police rest room to copy the drawing of the murdered man's face. He was more or less undisturbed – occasionally a police constable came in to have a cup of tea, and once a lost child was brought in to wait for its mother – but the afternoon passed quietly and by the time John returned Alex had made the required three copies.

"What have ye been up tae, faither?" said Alex.

"Weel, I went up to Peter's to give him your drawing of yon queer dagger – I'm still sure I've seen a picture of one somewhere, mind. His son Willie will be going to a lecture at the Watt Institute this evening and he's promised tae tak it with him and show it to some of the teachers and look in the library. Peter went tae the infirmary earlier this afternoon tae check up on young Bali. He's no regained consciousness yet – but the doctors think it won't be long. Then I went down to the Exchange coffee house to see what the gossip was – and found it was me! Fat chance o' keeping Dod's identity secret. Near everyone kens aboot the wee boy wi' the orangy dug even if they dinna ken his name."

The wee boy in question was in the money, so after leaving the docks he bought two penny pies in the Greenmarket, one for himself and one for Shadow. He and the dog ate them while sheltering in the arcade under the Town House, called the Pillars. Dod had clearly been thinking about the monkey. He turned to Shadow and said, "Yon monkey likes fruit. We'll go and see if there's ony spilt oaranges outside Keillers'." James Keillor and son had been manufacturing marmalade "since 1797". Their current shop was at the top of Castle Street. There were no oranges in sight. He wrinkled his nose. He could smell marmalade from somewhere. He went into the High Street where the smell seemed stronger. "Can ye smell that?" he said to Shadow, "Whar's it coming frae?" Shadow began to move forwards, eventually vanishing up a close on the north side of the High

Street. And there was Keiller's "works", where they made the marmalade and jams. They found an open door from which the smell of boiling marmalade and jam was emanating. There were also several crates of oranges stacked up outside.

Yesterday Dod would probably just have pinched a couple and run off, but something had changed in him. Maybe it was just having money in his pocket (he still had 1/10d left after the two pies) which made stealing seem wrong: maybe it was the prospect of "something" being done for him and the suspicion that that might evaporate if he was caught stealing, but anyway he put his head round the door and shouted, "Is onyone there?"

"Aye, Mrs Keiller's here. Wha wants her?"

Mrs Keiller was a formidable looking lady of middle years. As she approached the smell of marmalade got stronger.

"Guidsakes, its a wee lad and a marmalade dug," she said. "What do you twa want?"

"Guid afternoon," said Dod, removing his cap. "I want tae buy a couple o' oaranges."

"We dinna sell oranges – just marmalade and jam," said Mrs Keiller. "What does a wee lad want oranges for? And how has a wee lad got money?"

"I want tae buy them for Captain Melville's monkey, Rodriguez," said Dod. "He's frae foreign parts and only gets tae eat epples when he's in Dundee. I thocht he might like an oarange – and I kent you use oaranges tae mak yer marmalade. I thocht there might be some spilt ones lying aroond, but there arny ony, and then I saw thae braw looking ones."

"Well at least ye didna steal them," said Mrs Keiller.

"I micht hae done if I'd nae money," said Dod looking at his feet, "but I've got 1/10d left from running messages for Baillie Sma' and Deacon Davie and it didnae seem richt tae steal wi' money in ma pooch."

"Weel," said Mrs Keiller. "I like your honesty. "As I said we dinna sell oranges, but here's twa for free. I hope your monkey likes them."

She handed Dod two of the largest oranges she could find in the top crate. Dod thanked her, stuffed them into his coat pockets, replaced his cap and was just calling Shadow, who was exploring the smells coming from the boiling coppers, to heel when he was called back.

"Here's a jar o' marmalade for your Ma – ye do hae a Ma?"

"Oh aye," said Dod, accepting the marmalade with a slight bow. "Thank ye kindly Mistress Keiller. I'll tell abody what a fine wumman you are."

"There's a strange young man," said Elizabeth Keiller half to herself. "He'll either end up making a fortune or in jail!", and she returned to her boiling marmalade.

The pair headed up the Murraygate. They then turned up the Wellgate, being careful to pass Mr Niven's shop quickly and finally walked up the Hilltown to his room. His mother was out.

"She must have gone tae work after a'," he said to Shadow. So he left the marmalade, and a penny loaf he had bought, on a high shelf where his mother would see them but the mice couldn't reach. He decided that is was unlikely that the Captain would bring Rodriguez with him to the Smalls, so he hid the oranges, and a shilling, in a hole in the plaster concealed behind a small cupboard in far corner of the room. As far as he knew his mother had never found the hiding place. He then headed out again. It was beginning to get dark and he suddenly realised that he had not been to warn Mrs

Small of Captain Melville's visit, so he made his way as quickly as possible back down the hill and across towards the West Port.

His route took him along Bell Street and, as luck would have it, he ran into John and Alec as they were leaving the police station.

"Maister Sma', I've been doon tae the docks," and he recounted the events of the morning, ending up with the announcement that the Smalls were about to get a visit from Captain Melville.

"We'd better get back and warn Mrs Small then," said John.

"But ye'er ganging the wrang wey," said Dod, as they began to walk back along Bell Street in the direction of the town centre.

"We're going tae the Post Office in Reform Street," replied John. "I want to post this letter." and he took the letter he had written earlier that morning, inserted one of the drawings Alec had just made and sealed the envelope.

"And before you ask,", he said. "I'm not telling you who I'm writing to. If I'm wrong it won't matter and if I'm right, you'll all find oot."

Alec and Dod walked a few paces behind John. The two boys were wary of each other. Alex was a bit jealous of Dod's sudden appearance in his family and the praise that had been showered on him since last night; Betsey had been talking of nothing else all day. Dod was acutely aware that he was wearing Alec's cast off clothes and that Alec was a boy who had all the things Dod craved – a family, school and a guaranteed place in society. The ice was broken by Shadow, who rubbed up against Alex and began to lick his hand.

"That's a braw dug you've got, Dod. We've only got a cat, and she's really Betsey's," said Alec.

"Cats are fine tae," said Dod, somewhat unenthusiastically and launched into a description of Captain Melville and, particularly, his monkey. This clearly impressed Alec who countered by describing the events of the morning and Betsey's part in saving her mother.

"That man's worse than we thocht," said Dod. "Yer faither said I had tae be careful, but I didna expect him tae attack wimmen and children."

"We've a' been kept off the school till he's caught," said Alec. "And mither has been told to keep the door locked."

By the time they finally reached the Smalls' house, the boys were, if not yet friends, at least easy with each other. They knocked on the door and were answered by Betsey.

"Password!" she asked.

"Pencil," said John, playing along. "Or maybe it should be "sair bum"!"

Betsey opened the door and they all went into the kitchen where the rest of the family were gathered. John told Elizabeth of the immanent arrival of James Melville.

"I'm affy sorry Mistress Sma'. I should hae come and telt ye sooner."

"Dinna worry, Dod," she replied. "there's always someone unexpected coming to tea aroond here. Is the gossip true? Is he affy handsome?"

"I dinna ken. I suppose so," said Dod. "He's got a braw monkey though!"

Meanwhile Shadow and the Smalls' cat were eyeing each other up, much as the two boys had done half an hour earlier. Eventually the cat decided that Shadow was not sufficiently interesting and returned to its customary place by the fire. Shadow settled down at Dod's feet. Now that John had returned, Elizabeth sent the servant girl down to the shop to bring back a selection of cakes. Betsey helped her set the kitchen table and they all sat down to wait for the appearance of Captain Melville.

Chapter 8

In which Captain Melville visits the Smalls

The Captain knocked on the door at exactly five o'clock. John answered the door.

"Captain Melville, good of you to come,", said John. "I'm John Small."

"Please, call me James," replied the Captain. "I've seen you often about the town and indeed know you as a good friend to the maritime community. I am intrigued by the case you've got involved in. I couldn't not come!"

They walked together into the kitchen.

"Captain James Melville," said John. "My wife Elizabeth, daughter Betsey and my sons Alec, Tom and George. Dod you have already met."

Captain Melville swept off his hat and kissed Elizabeth's hand. He then bowed to Betsey and nodded to the boys.

"Good evening, Mrs Small, Betsey, boys," he said.

"Guid evening, Captain,", said Dod. "I don't suppose you've brocht Rodriguez wi' you?"

"I do not walk the streets of Dundee with a monkey on my shoulder!" said James. "Not even a superior and intelligent monkey like Rodriguez. You'll just have to visit the ship if you want to see him again.

"I'd like that fine," said Dod, "But will yer men let me on and can Shadow come on board and meet Rodriguez?"

"I will instruct my crew to give permission to a small boy to board the ship as long as he is accompanied by an orangy-brown dog," said James in a solemn voice.

Dod had had little experience of teasing. Most people who spoke to him meant exactly what they said – and were usually telling him what to do. But he was beginning to realise that these folk he was mixing with now were a bit different and he would have to adapt.

Betsey nudged him. "He's pulling your leg," she whispered.

By this time they were all seated at the table The tea had been brewed and a whole boiled ham brought in from the pantry. There were also hard boiled eggs and jars of Elizabeth's pickles, cakes and butter and jam and since the Smalls were bakers there was, as Dod described it later to his mother "breid like onything!". John said grace and eating commenced. For Dod eating was a chancy affair. He ate when he could – if he could – and it took all his will power not to grab at everything on the table, and to shove some in his pockets. He had never drunk tea out of a china cup before and had rarely eaten cakes or sandwiches off a plate. He watched Betsey and Alec carefully and tried to imitate their table manners.

"How did you become a Captain?" asked Tom. "Does it tak a long time?"

"My father was a Captain". said James, "Captain and owner of the *Providence*. It was a small ship, called a sloop, and he mainly did the coastal run from the Fife coalfields to Dundee. I went to sea at fourteen, as soon as I'd left school – first as an apprentice, and then at nineteen I became an ordinary seaman. I first sailed as a ship's Master at twenty one. When my father died there was only me and my sister left. We sold the *Providence* and managed to buy the *Oxalis*. She's a 78 ton, two masted schooner, if you're interested, and we do the continental runs now to the Baltic ports and France and Holland."

"Dae ye ever get attacked by pirates?" piped up George.

"I'm pleased to say that I have never encountered a pirate ship, Master George, but if we did Rodriguez would take care of them," replied the Captain, giving the other children a broad wink.

"That's enough, bairns," said John. "Captain Melville and I have to talk in private. Get ben the hoose for half an oor. Betsey, you can show Dod aroond."

After showing Dod the room where she slept, the boys bedroom and the apprentices' room, each of which was as large as Dod's entire apartment, they ended up in what John Small called, with tongue firmly in cheek, his "study". It was a small room, smelling strongly of pipe smoke, with a desk, an armchair a bureau and several bookshelves filled with books.

"Guidsakes, whit an affy lot o' books," exclaimed Dod.

"Faither is very fond of his books," replied Betsey.

"Oh look," said Dod, clearly excited. "He's got a' of Mr Dickens' books. I've read bits of "Oliver Twist", but

I've never managed tae find the end parts. I wonder if yer faither would let me read it?"

"Well," said Betsey, "he's aye trying tae get us tae read books – so I suppose he would. You'll have to ask him. You'd probably have to read them here though."

John, James Melville and Elizabeth were alone in the kitchen. The Captain took the paper Dod had left with him out of his pocket,

"The language is Hindi," he said. "I found a lascar who spoke good English and who could translate. This is what the words mean: "rakhana chupa" means keep hidden, "meeree pita" means my father, Kumpani means exactly what it sounds like – Company and "lnama" means reward. So I'm guessing that the young man you rescued gave you something for safe keeping – and that he is probably quite important. Maybe also that the East India Company is involved."

"Thanks very much James. You've got it just about right."

John then gave James a full account of what had happened over the last two days. He had already had some of the story from Dod, but the attack on Mrs Small was news as of course was Betsey's exploit with the toasting fork.

"Come through to my study," said John, "I want to show ye something."

After displacing Betsey and Dod who returned to the kitchen, John opened his bureau, pressed a hidden button and released a secret drawer. From this he produced the packet, unwrapped it and displayed the emerald."

"Good Heavens, I can see now what the stakes are – that emerald is worth a fortune. This man is much more dangerous than I thought. I think you and your family are still in danger."

"Aye well, James. You'll keep this to yerself for now. I think I know how to find out who the murdered man was and, if I'm right, we'll know soon enough. When I get more hard information I'll send Dod down to your ship."

Chapter 9

In which Dod attends a theatrical performance

The events of the day had been exciting. Meeting Captain Melville and Rodriguez had been amazing but also a bit disturbing and having tea at a table with cups and saucers had taken a good deal of concentration. Dod left the Smalls' house about seven o'clock and walked back towards the Hilltown. He didn't really feel like going home yet and was going slowly up the Nethergate when he noticed that there was a play about to start in Giles Penny Gaff in the Nethergate Quarry. This was a small brick built building where Mr Giles put on entertainments for the reasonable price of one penny for adults – a ha'penny for children. The billboard announced:

The terrible tragedy of Macbeth, King of Scots
By William Shakespeare
The part of the King to be played by Mr William
McGonagall
The eminent Dundee tragedian

Now Dod had heard of William Shakespeare, but had never seen any of his plays. *Everyone* in Dundee had heard of Wullie McGonagall. He was a strange man – a handloom weaver who thought himself a great actor and took every opportunity to get up on a stage. A performance by McGonagall usually attracted a capacity audience – but not necessarily for the right reasons. Dod paid his ha'penny and he and Shadow began to go inside. The doorman stopped Dod and started to tell him that his dog would have to stay outside but Shadow, who was a much better actor than McGonagall, raised her eyes and gave a soft whimper.

"Oh, get in," the man said. "But mak share she stays quiet."

They entered the darkened room. There was a stage at the front with a slightly tattered curtain and a row of whale oil lamps lining its edge. The seating consisted of low wooden benches. Most of these were already occupied. Dod was about to start to wiggle his way to the front when Shadow gave a low growl. Dod stopped and looked round. As his eyes became accustomed to the low light he noticed a tall man with fair hair and side-whiskers sitting in the second row. The man turned his head in Dod's direction and his face was illuminated by the stage lights. Dod ducked behind a large man and whispered to Shadow.

"Aye, ye're right. It's him. We'd better no get too close."

However Dod wanted to see the play so he squeezed his way to the front keeping to the opposite side of the room from the Englishman. "It would be good tae get the police in," he thought. "Maybe I'll think o' something."

Suddenly there was a roll on a drum, the curtain was pulled to the side and the play started. The *Macbeth* that unfolded was not exactly the *Macbeth* that Shakespeare wrote or indeed the *Macbeth* that could be seen at the Theatre Royal in Castle Street – but then here the seats cost a penny and not two shillings. It was a cut down version, lasting about an hour. As Mr Giles described it, it was "*Macbeth* with the bluidy bits left in."

The first scene was, of course, the three witches. There was clearly no lack of makeup in Mr Giles' company because the witches had eerie green complexions and huge noses bristling with warts. Long straggly hair, pointed hats and robes decorated by the sun and moon completed their outfits. After much toil and trouble round a cauldron, Macbeth – McGonagall entered to great cheers and was proclaimed "King hereafter". This was accompanied by much waving of his sword and pacing up and down the stage. The next scene was the arrival of King Duncan. He was played by a very old actor who, after being welcomed by Lady Macbeth, doddered round the stage and eventually lay down on a bed to sleep.

"Ye'd better hurry up Macbeth," shouted a wag in the audience, "or he'll dee in his bed afore ye can murder him!"

Macbeth and Lady Macbeth duly entered and there was much declaiming and waving of daggers in the air. The dastardly deed was finally done and a good deal of blood (pig's blood – Dod hoped) appeared on Duncan's nightgown. The curtain was drawn and the first "act" was over. Dod was naturally finding Shakespeare's language a bit difficult to understand and McGonagall was not making it any easier by his delivery, but the plot was clear and since it was all new to him he was quite enjoying it.

Banquo's murder came next and Dod's interest focussed on the boy who played Fleance. "He looks aboot my age," he thought. "I wonder whit it's like tae be an actor?" The banquet scene when Banquo's ghost appeared and Macbeth began to go mad gave McGonagall plenty of opportunity to show his acting abilities. The parade of future Kings was a bit of a cheat, thought Dod, Three actors kept going off stage left and returning stage right wearing a different hat! Lady Macbeth's hand washing scene was good. Dod had already realised that the actor playing her was the best, or possibly the only real, actor in the troupe. All too soon the final act arrived. Birnam wood had come to "high Dunsinnan hill" (which, Dod's neighbour whispered, "was jist up the Carse") and the fight between Macbeth and Macduff was about to start. This was McGonagall's great scene - the one his friends and his hecklers had come to see. The two men squared up. McGonagall spoke the immortal lines "lay on Macduff" and the sword fight began. Now McGonagall was well known for being reluctant to "die" so the fight carried on for much longer than Shakespeare intended, to the great delight of the cheering (and booing) audience. Finally Macbeth fell to his fatal wound but continued to writhe about on the floor waving his sword.

"He's died but he'll no lie doon," whispered the neighbour.

Suddenly the cheers and shouts were cut through by an English voice saying, "You couldn't act your own death if you were hanging at the end of a rope!"

Dod realised this was his chance and, diving to the back of the room shouted in his deepest voice, "Ye canna talk tae the King o' Scots like that, Englishman!" Someone shouted, "The mannie's right, yon McGonagall couldna act himsel' oot o' a paper poke." More voices were raised for and against the acting abilities of the Great Tragedian until finally a fist was swung and a general riot ensued. This was exactly what Dod had hoped for. He ran out and shouted, "Police, there's a fecht in the gaff!" When he heard the sound of a police whistle he went back inside but couldn't see much because Mr Giles had put out most of the stage light to avoid his theatre catching fire. His eyes gradually became used to the dark and it looked like his quarry had vanished.

"There must be an exit behind the stage," he thought.

Jumping up he collided with "Fleance".

"Did a big mannie wi' blond hair rin oot this wey?" asked Dod.

"Aye," said the other boy. "He knocked doon Mr McGonagall and went oot the back door. Is he yer faither or something?"

"No," said Dod, feeling important. "He's a murderer and a thief and he attacked ane o' the Baillies yesterday. I jist shouted fur the police, but they'll be too late. I'm Dod, by the way."

"Patrick," said the boy. "But how dae you ken a' that," he continued in a distinctly suspicious tone. So Dod recounted the events of yesterday, or at least the ones in which he had a starring role. Patrick was suitably impressed and Dod, realising that he might as well forget about the tall Englishmen for the time being, began to quiz Patrick about being an actor.

"Its no a bad job, I suppose," he said. "Macbeth's a good play fur me because Ah dinna get kilt. In an affy loat o' plays the boy or girl - I play both - gets kilt or dees and it's an affy trachle lying quiet fur half an oor while the ither actors are talkin' above ye. Ye canny move or sneeze or cough. Ah played "Little Nell" frae Mr Dickens *Curiosity Shop* a couple o' month ago. There's an affy lang death scene in that. Na, actin's no sae bad but when ah get alder Ah'm gaein' tae be a sojer."

Mr McGonagall had recovered from his encounter, had changed back into his normal clothes and was preparing to leave.

"That wiz a bra performance," said Dod, "Ah'll come back and see ye again."

"Thank you kindly, young sir. My interpretation of the Bard's famous characters are renowned all over Dundee, and I am known as far as Edinburgh." He swept off his bonnet, bowed and left.

"Ah didna want tae hurt the puir man," remarked Dod, "But Ah dinna think the world'll hear much mair o' him - "renowned" indeed!" In which judgement, as we all know, Dod was seriously wrong.

Chapter 10

In which Dod talks to his mother and meets Willie David

The next day was Friday and nothing much seemed to be happening. Dod continued to ask around the town and found that a few people did recognise the blond stranger, but no-one had seen him for the last two days. Either he was keeping out of sight, or he had changed his appearance. Dod felt instinctively that it would be better not to rush down to the *Oxalis* immediately, but maybe wait a day – he had found from experience that it didn't do to pester people. For the same reason he had decided not to visit the Smalls till the next day. He hadn't left till seven last night and was acutely aware that he had hardly seen his mother for the last couple of days. During the day he had taken some of his hidden money and bought some wood and a bag of coals and dragged them up the stairs to their room. He then went out again and bought a couple of meat pies from Mr Niven in the Wellgate. Mr Niven looked at him curiously.

"Aye," he said, "I've heard about your antics. Maybe you'll mak something o' yourself yet. Here's a couple o' sausages – they're no the freshest, but they willna kill you. I'll be eating the same ones for ma ain tea. Oh and here's a bone fur yir wee dug."

"Thanks affy, Mr Niven," said Dod, rushing off with the pies and sausages before Mr Niven changed his mind.

"Guidsakes," he said to himself or to Shadow – there was really no difference. "Things have really changed if Mr Niven is civil tae me. I suppose Mr David must hae telt him."

By the time his mother returned from the factory Dod had a fire going and was heating the pies on a griddle and starting to fry the sausages. However as soon as Jeannie entered it was obvious she was not in a good mood.

"Whar did ye get the money for that, and what's thae claes yer wearin'?"

"I did Baillie Sma' a bit o' a service," said Dod, who had not yet told his mother the whole story, "and he gave me a shilling and some o' his son Alec's claes."

"Yer takin' charity noo, are ye, wearin' ither fowks cast offs. Do they no think yer mother can claethe her ain son?" spat out Jeannie.

"That's no fair, mither," he said, "Alec is a year alder than me and a guid bit bigger. If I hadna got them they would hae gone tae his wee brother. They're only second hand, the anes I took aff were aboot sixth hand."

"It'll dae ye nae guid, mixing wi' the toun gentry. Ye'll be getting ideas above yer station. I should nivver hae let ye leave the mill. Ye'll end up in the jail at this rate."

"That's what Mistress Keillor said," said Dod, "Except she also said that I micht mak my fortune! By the by it was her that sent ye that pot o' marmalade"

"Baillie Sma', Mistress Keillor! Wha else hae ye been getting in wi'?"

"Well," said Dod, "there's Mr Davie, wha ye ken. Oh and Captain Melville, o' the schooner *Oxalis*," with more than a little pride in his voice.

Jeannie was lost for words and began to eat one of the pies that she had earlier complained about. Now that she was quieter Dod proceeded to describe most of the events of the last two days, leaving out the monkey and assuming that his mother would not ask about Mrs Keillor. Jenny just sat there, eating her pie and sausage and shaking her head wordlessly.

"Ye must tak efter yer grandfaither, mixing wi' the gentry," she mumbled between mouthfuls.

"Baillie Sma's no gentry," said Dod. "He's whit's cried a self made man. Alec telt me that his grandfaither was just a quarryman at the Kingoodie quarries and," he lowered his voice, "Alec also telt me that his Auntie Jean has twa lads like me who hae nae faithers, although I dinna think he's supposed tae ken."

"Ah weel," said Jean, having apparently got over her anger. "Ye'll gang yer ain gait as usual, I expect. Jist dinna forget yer auld mither."

"Guidsakes, mither, your're no auld. Yer no yet thirty. Ye could easily get a man if ye wanted to."

Dod had blurted this last sentence out and now went bright red. However Jeannie just looked sadly at him,

"I still love yer faither," she whispered, "even after a this time. I still think he micht send for us when his faither dies and he taks ower the ferm."

Dod shook his head at this silliness. He was sure that his father would never send for them. He just wished his mother would get over it like he had done and start living for herself. He even meant it about her getting married – as long as he approved of the man, of course. However Jessie was now turning a bit maudlin and reached for the whiskey bottle.

"I'm fair wabbit," she said half to herself. "Just a drop at the end o' the day," and although he hated to see her drunk, Dod could understand the way she felt from his own experiences in the spinning works. It was best just to leave for a while.

"Ah'm gaein' oot tae hae a wee look roond," he said," Maybe someone's needing a message run." And he went down the stairs, through the back courts and into the street. He walked down the Hilltown and into the Wellgate but met no-one he recognised and no-one who needed a message delivered.

Half an hour later he was back and was about to return home when he was hailed by Willie David, Peter David's son,

"Hey, Dod," he shouted. "I've found oot what yon dagger is and where it comes frae. Come up to the hoose with me and I'll tell you all together."

"Thanks, Willie," said Dod. "I'd like that fine. There's nothing happening oot here on the street tonight."

The pair went up the close and into Peter David's house.

"Faither, Mither," said Willie. "I've found oot about yon dagger that Alec Small made a drawing of. I met Dod in the street outside so I've brought him up to hear about it too."

"Sit doon and hae yer tea first," said Isabella. "How about you. Dod, have ye eaten?"

"Thank ye kindly, Mistress Davie, but I have had my tea," said Dod reluctantly, as he found turning down a free meal very difficult.

"Never mind, ye'll hae a scone and jam while Willie eats his." And she placed a plate with a couple of scones in front of him and indicated the butter and jam already on the table.

"Right," said Willie, "It took me some time, but I eventually found a picture of the dagger in ane of the books in the Institute library. Its ca'd a katar and is very common in India."

"That figures," said Dod with his mouth full of scone. "Bali looks bit like the lascars frae the boats and they're Indian."

"Aye, "said Peter, "Diprose and Bali were waiting for a jute boat to arrive. But we're still not sure who the packet belongs to although I'm beginnin' tae think it must be Bali. Its ower late tae be disturbing John with this information. You can gae round tae see him the morns morn, Willie. Ye can tak Dod wi' ye tae keep him oot o' mischief. Unless ye'd something else planned, Dod"

"Weel I was going tae go doon tae the docks tae see the Captain's monkey," said Dod. "But that can wait till the efternoon. Whit time are ye gaein roond, Willie?"

"Its best to wait till the shop has calmed doon a bit and John has time to speak to ye," said Peter. "How aboot you meet outside the close at half past nine. That wey ye'll get there aboot ten. By the by did ye ken there was a fun fare in toun this week – wi' a menagerie. There's supposed tae be an elephant."

"Oh that would be grand, Maister Davie. I've never seen an elephant before," said Dod jumping up excitedly. I'd better gae hame noo. I'll see you tomorrow Willie."

Chapter 11

In which Dod meets an erudite gentleman

The next morning Dod was up early. Jeannie had already left for the mill so he lit a small fire and made himself a cup of tea and had it with a scone he had secreted in his pocket from last night's tea at the Davids'. By half past nine he was waiting, as instructed, at the close mouth of Peter David's tenement. A couple of minutes later Willie emerged. Although the two had known each other to nod to since shortly after Dod had arrived in Dundee, the age difference meant that they did not really know each other well. In the last few months, because Dod had been running more and more messages for Peter David he had been thrown into the company of his son more often. Willie was eighteen years old and a bit taller than his father. Dod had picked up the facts that Willie was "bright" and "ambitious". He knew Willie attended night classes at the Watt Institute, but had no idea what this entailed.

"Hi Willie," said Dod. "Ye dinna mind me coming alang tae Maister Sma's. If ye dinna want tae be trachled wi' a wee boy I can just go on my own and meet ye there."

"Dinna be daft, Dod. I'd like yer company fine. Faither thinks a lot of you. He says your the maist reliable wee messenger he's ever had. Even if you hadna got involved with this investigation I think he was thinking of geeing you a job in the firm when ye're alder. Anyway you can tell me all aboot this famous monkey. It seems to have made quite an impression on you."

So Dod launched into a description of his meeting with Captain Melville's Rodriguez which lasted all the way down the Hilltown and into the junction of the Wellgate with Baltic Street where they headed west along Bell Street. As they reached the junction with Constitution Road, Willie suddenly said, "That's the Watt Institute, just down the street there – the second building on the right."

"What dae ye learn there," asked Dod. "I've heard the name but I ken nothing aboot it."

"Well," said Willie, "It's a bit of a mixture. There's a library, where I found the book with the picture of the dagger. There's a wee museum with stuffed animals and birds and odd things people have given them. But most important for me, they have evening classes. I'm learning aboot engineering and mining. I want to go to America when

I'm alder. There's lots of opportunity there. See, if we've got time I could tak you intae the museum if you want."

"I'd like that fine," said Dod. "I think Maister Sma' can wait another half an oor, especially as he's no expecting us!"

They first had to get past the door-keeper.

"Good morning, Mr Taylor, I'm just taking young Dod here for a look round the museum if you don't mind. Dod often runs errands for my father. He was round the house last night when I got back from my class and when I told him there was a museum he wanted to see it."

Mr Taylor might have baulked at the idea of some members bringing in a boy who was clearly not from the respectable working class, but Willie was well known at the Institute and, more importantly, he knew Willie was Peter David's son and the Trades were important financiers of the Watt Institute.

"Aye weel, make sure he keeps his haunds aff the exhibits," said Mr Taylor. "They dinna look too clean tae me!"

"The cheek," said Dod as they climbed the stairs to the museum. "They were washed yesterday!"

The museum was not large, but it contained an eclectic collection of objects donated by Dundee's upper and middle classes – especially her sea Captains. There were stuffed animals, rocks, shells and exotic weapons from all the countries where a Dundee ship had traded. Dod immediately rushed over to very realistic stuffed mongoose battling with a large cobra.

"Wha won yon fecht, I wonder," he shouted.

"Very likely the mongoose," said a voice from the other side of the glass cabinet. The voice materialised into a man with a shock of rather unkempt curly hair wearing a pair of gold pince-nez.

"We didna' mean to disturb you, Mr Lindsay," said Willie. "I was just showing the museum to young Dod, here. I'm afraid he got a bit excited."

"No harm in that," said James Bowman Lindsay. "Better to be excited about life than go through it in a state of boredom."

Turning to Dod. "Mongooses are used to kill poisonous snakes in India. I imagine they are related to weasels and stoats here."

Leading the boys over to a large stone with strange markings on it he said, "What do you think of that then?"

Dod peered at the object. "I dinna ken, maybe the one at the top's a floor – sorry a flower; and then there's two circles joined together. Oh and surely that's a comb at the bottom.

"Very good. Very good indeed. These stones were carved by the inhabitants of Scotland who were here when the Romans arrived. They are often called the Picti, or painted people, because they tattooed themselves. There are hundreds of these stones all over the east of Scotland and nowhere else in the world. We think that the symbols are a language – but no-one knows what it means."

"Are you trying tae find oot, Mr Lindsay," asked Dod.

"Not really, but I am making a dictionary of all the known languages in the world – it's taking a long time though."

"Mr Lindsay is daeing more than that," said William, "He's trying tae send telegraphs without wires – through the air. Jist think what that would mean. Ye could talk tae people on ships – and in America!"

"That's also taking its time," said Lindsay. "But William is right to say that it would change the world if it could be done. When an event happens in India, for example, we have to wait for the news to arrive by ship, and even the fastest tea clippers take more than two months."

"We'd better go now, Mr Lindsay, we were supposed tae be at Baillie Small's aboot half an oor ago."

"I heard he had a bit of trouble a day or two ago – Oh *you're* the boy everyone is talking about. Let me shake your hand. If you ever think I can be of use, I live in Union Street – anyone will tell you where."

The boys left Mr Lindsay poring over some mineral specimens and went out and down the staircase. Back in the street they were greeted wildly by Shadow.

"Ye'd think we'd been awa for a month instead o' half an oor," said Dod.

They carried on along towards the West Port. Dod was interested in the carved stones and asked Willie if he knew any more about them.

"All I know is that there are a few round Glamis, where my family came from. Apparently there's an affy famous one near Aberlemno which marks the place where thae Pict fowk beat the English."

By this time they had reached the bakehouse.

"Hello, Mr Small," said Willie. "We've come tae tell ye what the dagger is and tae find oot if there's any mair information."

"Well, Willie – and Dod – and Dod's dug – there *is* new information. I've received a telegram from London. Something Henry Ogilvie said made me think that Mr Diprose might be working for the East India Company – they often refer to it as "John Company" among themselves – so I sent one of Alec's drawings to them yesterday. Sure enough, Diprose was from the Company and they are sending someone up on the train on Monday."

"That maks perfect sense, Mr Small, the dagger is Indian it's called a katar and its pretty handy I'd think."

"Come up tae the hoose," said John. "It's near dinner time and Mrs Small maks pea soup on Saturday, besides Betsey is always asking after Dod - or maybe its just yer dug she likes!"

After they had eaten, John took Dod into his "study", Once his pipe had been successfully lit he finally turned his attention to the matter at hand.

"I've just had word from the Infirmary," he said. "Bali is conscious and able to speak, I'd like you tae go up and talk tae him. It will be less intimidating than either me or

Peter and I certainly don't want the first person he sees tae be Angus McLeod – his heart may be in the right place, but he aye pits his muckle great foot in it!"

John stopped to laugh at his own joke and take a couple of drags on his pipe.

"Here's a letter for Mrs Mitchell, the Matron. Ye'll have tae hand it tae the porter on the main door. When ye get tae see Bali, start by explaining to him that I am one of the most important people in the toun. Its an exaggeration, but it will give him confidence that he gave his packet tae the right person. Tell him its safe and that I have contacted the East India Company. Watch for his reaction. If the packet really belongs to him he'll be pleased by this news. Ye can also let him know that I suggest that he does not go back tae Mistress Ogilvie's but comes tae stay here. Oh and try and find oot what ye can of the robbery without upsetting him. I'm sure ye'll know what tae say – tell him about the monkey and yer dug. He's a bit alder than you but he's still a boy."

Chapter 12

In which Dod goes to the Infirmary and speaks to Bali

Half an hour later Dod presented his letter to the porter on duty at the Infirmary. He knew the Infirmary well, it was just to the east of the Hilltown, on King Street. He had been in it himself as an outpatient when he hurt himself at the spinning mill. It had a good reputation among the workers of Dundee, although it was a bit small for the expanding population and Dod had heard rumours that they were going to build a bigger one somewhere to the west of the Hilltown. He supposed the Deacon would know all about that. He sat and waited while another porter took his letter to the Matron. Shadow, of course, had to stay outside. The porter returned. Giving him an evil look – he clearly disapproved of small boys – he motioned Dod to get up.

"Matron will see you," he said. "Follow me."

Matron got up from behind her desk and scrutinised Dod.

"You look clean enough," she said, "Still you had better wash your hands before going into the ward. Now Bali has only been conscious since this morning so you can have exactly fifteen minutes with him – and say nothing to excite him. Nothing about the attacks on Mr Small and his family, nothing about you exploits – brave though they were." and here Matron actually smiled.

They went into the corridor.

"Nurse, take Mr Johnson to the men's ward and show him to Bali's bed. He's to have exactly fifteen minutes."

Dod sat down next to Bali who slowly opened his eyes. He slowly focused on a boy a few years younger than himself who looked clean – Bali was fastidious – but not particularly tidy.

"Who are you?" he said.

"I'm called Dod, that's short for George, and I've been sent by Mr Small – he's the man wi' the red beard that saved you. Mr Small is a Baillie – that's a kind o' magistrate - and is a respected citizen. You can trust him."

"I have no choice," said Bali, "The only person I knew in your country is dead."

"Aye well, he told me to tell you two things. Firstly the packet is weel hidden and secondly he has written tae the East India Company and had a reply."

"Oh that is good," said Bali, clearly relieved. "They will help me return home. Not that it is not pleasant in Dundee, although a little cold, but my father will be worried if he hears no news."

"Is yer faither – sorry father, I must try to speak good English to you – some kind of Prince?"

"He is the Maharaja of a very small state in India – but it is a state that many would like to control – that is why the Company is so keen to help."

"Can you tell me what happened," asked Dod.

"The story is simple. The Company supplied a few officers to help train my father's soldiers in modern methods of warfare. One of these was Captain Fizjames, the man who attacked us. He stole the emerald from the main temple in our town, killing two of the priests to do so, and fled. We discovered that he had disguised himself as a lascar and taken a berth on one of the jute ships bound for Dundee – I'm sure he did not choose Dundee – it was just the first boat leaving. We, Mr Diprose and I, found places on a British frigate coming to England. This allowed us to arrive in Dundee ten days before Fitzjames. We saw him leaving the ship and followed him to the Sailors' Home – he arrived in disguise and left as the Fizjames that you know. We kept following him and finally accosted him in the dark street where Mr Small found us. Jasper drew his pistol and tried to arrest him. I was behind Fizjames and I was able to take the packet out of his pocket as the two men confronted each other. However, as you know, Fizjames was faster and stabbed Jasper in the heart. He turned round and saw me. He struck at me with Jasper's pistol which he had taken from his body. That is when my saviours turned up."

"Ah weel," said Dod. Ye're safe now and so is yer packet. Maister Small said to ask you if you would like to come and stay with them when ye're able to move. Mistress Small is affy nice and they have four children. Alec is a year older than me and Betsey is my age. I visit them a lot these days – and you could see my dog. Maybe when your better and this Fitzjames man has been caught I could show ye round Dundee. We could go and see Captain Melville and his monkey."

"You have a monkey in Dundee," said Bali. "That is quite a coincidence. You see the emerald was stolen from the Temple of Hanuman – and Hanuman is a monkey. He is one of our gods but he takes the shape of a monkey. I would like to meet this earthly incarnation of Hanuman – I have a feeling he may have a part to play before this adventure is finished."

The nurse arrived at Bali's bed.

"That's enough," she said. "The patient has to rest now. I hope you haven't been disturbing him!"

"Oh no. I am much relieved by what Dod has told me. I will sleep easier now."

Turning to Dod –"Tell Mr Small I will be delighted to come and stay with him until I am well enough to go home."

Dod and Bali solemnly shook hands as only boys can, and Dod left the ward. He walked along the corridor, said cheerio to the porter and was reunited with Shadow, who was sitting patiently on the steps of the Infirmary. Some sixth sense made him look round carefully. He suddenly noticed a flash of light from the entrance of Hospital Lane.

"There's a man standing there watching – and he's got a gold watch chain," he said to himself. "And your usual loiterers dinna have gold watch chains."

Dod nipped back into the Infirmary and addressed the porter.

"I've just seen the man that murdered Bali's friend. He's standing at the end of the lane. You'll easy recognise him – fair hair, mutton chops, checked troosers and a big watch-chain. Dinna let him in – and be careful, he's got a fair wicked knife and maybe a pistol. I'm going tae try and lead him aff."

He rushed, pointed at the shape which was still visible at the end of the lane, and said to Shadow. "Go and gie him a nip on the ankle."

Shadow ran off and a couple of second later a sharp cry emanated from the lane followed by the man who Dod now knew was called Fizjames and was a triple (at least) murderer.

"I'll kill you," he shouted, "You and your damned dog!"

"Heel, Shadow," shouted Dod, and ran round the side of the Infirmary. Through the Infirmary grounds, over the back wall, across Bucklemaker Wynd - a little hesitation to make sure Fizjames could see where they were going - then through the orchards of Forebank house, across the Bowling Green and, having led him far enough away from the Infirmary, they disappeared in the back courts of the Hilltown. They seemed to have lost Fizjames, but Dod had no desire to take the risk of the man discovering where he lived, so they crossed the Hilltown to the west side and headed up Rosebank Street. They then veered west again, along Constitution Street. When he felt that Fizjames had been completely shaken off, they made their way cautiously down towards the Overgate and the Smalls' House.

Sitting once again in Mr Small's "study", Dod recounted his conversation with Bali and told of the sighting of Fizjames."

"You daft loon!", said John. "He could hae kilt you!"

"Oh no," Mr Sma', "There was nae chance that he could catch us. He was too slow and he disnae ken the toun like I do."

"Never the less," said John. " Ye could hae slipped, sprained yer ankle, gone under a cart – any number o' things – then he could have caught ye, and that knife would hae made short wark of you – and yer dug. Did ye think of what other people would feel if ye had got hurt – your mother, Betsey, Alec, Mrs Small – me? We've got quite tae like you, ye know. And besides, he knows what ye look like now – ye'll have tae be careful whenever ye're out till we catch him."

"Ah'm sorry, Mr Sma'. I didnae think. I jist wanted tae get him awa' frae the Infirmary. After all, he said," breaking into his usual grin. "I can rin faster than Bali – stuck in his bed."

"Well be careful when you go home. I'll send a note tae the Matron and suggest that we collect Bali tomorrow afternoon. He should be able to travel by then. I'll get a cab and we'll sneak him oot the back door."

It had been another long day for Dod. He left the house out the back of the close, through the back court and over the back wall. He went through a few more back courts and finally emerged from a close on the Scourinburn. He decided that they would go home through the lighted main streets – at least that way if Fizjames saw him, he would probably see Fizjames first, and even if he didn't there would be plenty of passers by to call to for help. He'd started thinking again. Like most boys of his age he was not particularly introspective, and the idea that John Small and his family would be affected – even hurt – by his death was a bit of a surprise. Of course he knew they were grateful for his intervention – but he had never really thought that they might have become attached to him. His mother loved him – at least he assumed she did – it was difficult to tell at times. Shadow loved him. But for the rest, as a small boy with a poor unmarried mother, he was at best tolerated. Certainly Mr David, and a few other men he ran errands for, sometimes gave him an extra penny. Sometimes they would ruffle his hair and ask after him or his mother, but he had no illusions about the fact that if he disappeared he would be replaced by another small boy. Now he had to think about the idea that people might like him for himself. He was getting to grips with this concept when Shadow gave a low growl. Instantly Dod slunk into a dark close-mouth and peered out carefully. Sure enough it was Fizjames, although without Shadow's warning growl Dod would not have recognised him. He was dressed in a long black coat and had a soft hat pulled down over his face. He must have realised that his description was rapidly circulating round the town. More interestingly, he was not walking alone. He was in deep conversation with a smaller man. Dod could not be sure, but by his dress the companion might be a sailor or a fisherman.

"That's more than likely," he thought, "He canna easily leave Dundee by train. The safest thing he could do would be to tak' a boat down the coast where he wouldna be recognised."

Remembering Mr Small's concerns about his safety, Dod decided not to follow the two men. It was getting very dark and they were clearly heading away from the lighted main streets towards the docks.

"Come on, Shadow. Home. I've got just the thing planned for the morrow's morn!"

Chapter 13

In which Dod meets Rodriguez again

This Sunday was one of Jeannie's "Kirk Sundays". In other words she had decided to attend church. She alternated between calling ministers, elders and the like all the names in the day, based on her experiences with them after Dod's birth, and going through a religious phase. She was currently in one of these and was dressing in her best clothes when Dod and Shadow woke. She tried as usual to persuade Dod to accompany her but, as usual, he declined. The main problem with the Kirk (apart from the long sermons and hard pews) was the fact that Shadow was not allowed in. He could just about see why libraries and museums and Infirmaries would keep dogs out, but why would the Kirk which was "open to all men" exclude dogs? Dogs, thought Dod, were men too. There was also the problem of all the different kirks. Jeannie went to the Kirk of Scotland; the Smalls to the Free Kirk. Some Irish boys he knew went to a completely different church – they called themselves Romans. It seemed odd to Dod that the same religion had so many different ways of worshipping. A niggling thought reminded him that the Smalls all went to Kirk - but he would deal with that if they ever suggested that he accompany them.

This morning he had more important things to do. He was finally going to take Rodriguez his oranges. Once Jeannie had left he moved the cupboard and removed the oranges from the hole in the wall where he had hidden them. While he was at it he checked that his shilling was still there. The oranges were still fine, which was not surprising since the hole in the outside wall was as good as the iceboxes that rich people had. Putting them in his pocket he called Shadow and the two went out, down the Hilltown, down the Wellgate and the Murraygate towards the docks. It was downhill all the way and, being a Sunday all the shops were shut, so there was no temptation to linger and the pair soon arrived at the William IV dock and the gangplank of the *Oxalis*.

"Is there onyone there?" shouted Dod, standing on the gangplank, but not risking going on board until he was invited.

"Aye, there's me," came a voice from onboard, followed by a tousled head. This belonged to a boy a few years older than Dod.

"Oh you must be the wee lad that the Captain telt me aboot. Come on board and bring yer dug. The Captain was very particular that the dug could come aboard too."

"She's ca'ed Shadow," said Dod. "And I'm Dod."

"Jim," said the boy. "Apprentice sailor, and man of a' work!"

"It must be a grand life," said Dod.

"Aye weel, it usually is, but you wouldna say so if ye were caught in a gale and had tae try and get the sail doon."

Jim opened the door of the Captain's cabin and the two boys went in.

"There's Rodriguez, up on top of the cabinet there. Have ye got something for him tae eat?"

"Aye, I've got a couple of oaranges that I got frae Mrs Keiller."

"I can see that you could charm ladies of a certain age," said Jim. "You and yer dug! Did she no try and get the dug tae advertise her marmalade – she's the right colour!"

"Hmph," said Dod, not happy at the way the conversation was going. "Do I peel the oarange?"

"No ye can jist gie it tae him as it is. He can peel it himsel'. If he's in a bad mood he micht throw the peel at you!"

Meanwhile Rodriguez was studying Shadow closely. In his experience dogs were chancy creatures. Some of them were all right, but others would bark at you or even try to nip you. Until he knew to which type Shadow belonged he would keep his distance. Still oranges were among his favourite fruits so he took the risk and jumped down on the desk and took the orange from Dod's hand, keeping his eyes firmly on Shadow all the time. He then retreated back to his perch on top of the cabinet and began to peel the orange. Suddenly Rodriguez threw a bit of peel at Shadow. Shadow pricked up her ears and gave Dod a quick glance. Getting no response she sank back into the pleasant doze from which she had been woken. This was strange behaviour for a dog thought Rodriguez. He should explore further. He jumped down on the table and offered both Dod and Jim segments of his orange. He then jumped on Dod's shoulder and began to search through his hair.

"Whit's he daeing?" exclaimed Dod.

"He's looking for fleas or nits – or even grains of salt, according tae the Captain."

"I dinna think I've got fleas," said Dod. "At least no' many."

He appeared to be right, because Rodriguez soon tired of Dod's hair and jumped on Shadow's back and started to rake through her fur. There seemed to be better hunting there.

"Probably fleas," said Dod. "She's usually got a few fleas."

Finally, finished with Shadow, Rodriguez jumped back on the table and offered his paw to first Dod and then Jim to shake. Then he jumped back to his normal seat on the cupboard.

"He sure likes you – and yer dug – I've never seen him daeing that wi' a dug afore," said Jim.

The two boys left the cabin and went up on deck.

"Whar dae ye come frae," said Dod to Jim.

"Frae Fife," Jim replied, "My faither knows the Captain and got me taken on as an apprentice. Efter five years I can become a seaman and then, if I pass my examinations, maybe a mate."

"Examinations!," said Dod. "I didna ken ye needed tae pass examinations tae sail a ship."

"Oh aye," said Jim. "Ye need tae be able tae read charts and navigate. And ye hae tae have good colour vision tae be able tae read the flags properly."

"Weel," said Dod. "I can read and count and I can tell red frae green, so maybe I could jine the ship as an apprentice in a couple of years when you become a seaman."

"Maybe ye could," replied Jim, "The Captain seems tae like ye, and that's the main thing. By the way did ye really stick yer pencil point in yon lad's bum?" So Dod had to recount his exploits once again, finishing up with a description of Fizjames.

"If ye see him mooching round the docks, tell Captain Melville or send a boy tae Baillie Sma's – It'll be worth a penny or two. Anyway, I'd better get back noo. Ma mither will be back frae the Kirk and will be getting' the dinner ready. Do you jist stay on the ship?"

"Aye," said Jim. "When we're in port in Dundee. A' the ither sailors gae hame tae their families but I prefer tae stay here. Someone has tae be on board tae guard the ship – its braw and quiet, and I get peyed!"

"See ye later, then," said Dod and he and Shadow went down the gangplank and back towards the town.

He was right. Jeannie was back from the Kirk and feeling good about herself. This manifested itself in the production of a very respectable dinner consisting of a good plate of mince and tatties. She even refrained from drinking.

"I was thinkin'," she said. "Maybe you could write a letter tae yer grandfaither Johnson. Jist tae let him ken that ye can write. You could even tell him aboot yer exploits and that ye ken Baillies and suchlike. Maybe he would ask us back."

"I suppose I could," mused Dod, although he was much less keen on the idea of leaving Dundee for a farm than was his mother. Although he could remember little from his time before coming to Dundee, one memory had stuck in his mind. It was the winter before he left and he was sitting in the thatched cottage where he lived with his grandparents. It had just got dark outside and his grandmother came in frozen stiff and soaked to the skin from a day in the fields. She stoked up the fire and hung her wet clothes in front of it in a vain attempt to get them dry for tomorrow. The smoke from the fire set off her cough, which was always bad in the damp weather. She must have been in her mid forties, but she looked like an old woman. No, Dundee was no paradise, thought Dod, but it was better than life on the farm. The trouble was that when his mother thought about her former life she imagined herself as the Farmer's wife, not one of the labourers.

"But I'd better wait till this man Fizjames has been caught and the hale business has been tied up," he continued. "Which reminds me I've tae go wi' Baillie Sma' tae collect the Indian boy frae the Infirmary – he's a Prince, ye ken."

"Guidsakes," exclaimed Jeannie. "A Prince. As if Baillies and Sea Captains werna bad enough!"

And leaving Jeannie to her Sunday afternoon nap, Dod and Shadow set off for the Infirmary.

As he approached, Dod kept his eyes peeled for Fizjames, although he was fairly sure that Shadow would warn him. He had not to hang about for long when John Small arrived in a growler. This was a closed carriage which could comfortably take three people and a dog.

"Wait here and keep a look out," said John. "I won't be long."

Sure enough John and Bali emerged a few moments later. They were accompanied by the Matron who helped to settle Bali in the carriage. John got in next followed by Dod.

"Shadow can follow us," said Dod.

"Naw, she'd better come wi' us, We don't want to take the chance of Fizjames seeing her and guessing who is inside."

This statement was received by a disapproving look from Matron and a "Humph" from the driver. Still you did not argue with Baillie Small so Shadow got into a carriage for the first time in her life. She did not seem any happier than the cabby. It was bad enough having a monkey on your back but being bounced around in a contraption that smelt of horses was much worse. However the journey did not take long and they has soon climbed the stairs to the Smalls' flat where they were met by Elizabeth and four excited children. Bali was settled in Alec's room and Dod was dispatched in the coach, which had to return to the Railway Station where it usually waited for trade. From there he went to Mrs Ogilvie's lodging house in order to collect Bali's and Mr Diprose's belongings.

"They'll have a cart, or a wheelbarrow," said John, "Henry Ogilvie will help you. I think he'd like to see Bali anyway."

Chapter 14

In which Mr Richardson is put in his place

A letter arrived at the Smalls' house by the first post on Monday. Mr Richardson, of the East India Company, wrote to say that he would be arriving in Dundee on the five o'clock train from Edinburgh and would be staying at the Royal Hotel, opposite the City Churches. Could Prince Bali Ramakrishnan meet him there? John Small immediately sent a note to the Hotel explaining that the doctors has been quite explicit that Bali should have as much rest as possible for the next few days and inviting Mr Richardson to come to the Smalls' house at seven o'clock. There he could meet Bali and some of the people involved in the case. John had been worrying more and more about Dod's sighting of Fizjames. It was obvious that he could not remain in Dundee for very much longer – his description was now being circulated widely – but equally he would not leave without the emerald. Dod thought the man talking to Fizjames might be a fisherman – and his suggestion that Fizjames might be planning to escape by sea seemed very plausible. But if he was seriously arranging his departure he must have a plan for recovering the emerald. John went through in his mind all the people involved, to check that they were reasonably safe. His family, Peter's family and Captain Melville were fine. Dod could, and probably should, stay with them. Then it suddenly occurred to him that Dod's mother, Jeannie, could be in danger. Fitzjames could easily find out where Dod and his mother lived. But no, Fizjames was from the upper classes, he would not consider it possible that anything he did to a poor woman from the slums would persuade John to part with the emerald. Bali was the obvious target. Fizjames would eventually find out that he was living with the Smalls. Although they had good strong doors, it would not be a bad idea to ask Angus McLeod to station a policeman outside their door. He would see to that immediately.

The day passed slowly. John sent a note to Peter asking him to come round after tea to meet Mr Richardson, but did not think it worth bothering Captain Melville yet. Bali had insisted in getting up for a while after dinner after eating some of Mrs Small's pea soup (specially made without ham since she knew Bali was a vegetarian) and John felt it was time to tell him the whole story of what had happened since the attack. Something in the tone of Mr Richardson's letter made him think that events would move rapidly once he arrived. So the story of the attacks on Peter and John, of Dod and his pencil and of Bessie and the toasting fork were recounted. Bali was shown the emerald, but after holding it for a few moments gave it back to John for safe keeping.

"This man will not give up till he is caught," he said. "The stakes are too high. He has killed in India. He has killed here – and worse he has killed a Company man. His only way of avoiding justice is to steal back the emerald and use the fortune it will realise to change his identity. I cannot thank you enough for what you have done for me. You will all be well rewarded."

"Never mind about that just now. The important thing is for you to rest and get your strength back. We will continue to search for Fizjames. I think you are right – none of us will be safe until he is caught. Mr Richardson, from the Company, should be here about seven o'clock. Until then you should get some more sleep."

Not unexpectedly Dod turned up at the Smalls in time for tea. He played "snap" with Alec, Betsey and George for a while and then, borrowing a copy of "David

Copperfield" he announced that he was going to sit with Bali for a while. Meanwhile Peter arrived and he, John and Elizabeth sat in the kitchen and waited for the arrival of Mr Richardson, while the children were banished to Betsey's room. At ten past seven there was a loud rap on the door. John opened it and the policeman announced "A gentleman to see you, Mr Small." and presented a stout gentleman, expensively dressed and carrying a silver topped cane which he had clearly just used to announce his presence.

"Mr Richardson," said John, "Please come in." Holding out his hand, "John Small, and this is my wife Elizabeth and my friend Peter David, Would you like some refreshment – a dram of whiskey, or some of Mrs Small's home made lemonade?"

"Thank you, no. I will just collect the Prince and the emerald and go. I want to be back in London by Tuesday night."

"I think that would be very unwise in the light of the doctor's instructions," said John. "Indeed I would be reluctant to see Bali moved from here. Fizjames is still at liberty and he is far safer here than in the Royal Hotel. You will have noted the presence of a policeman outside the door.

Perhaps you should hear the whole story of what has happened since we first encountered Bali."

"I do not need advice from a baker, Small. No doubt you are concerned about the reward – it will be paid once the emerald is back in the hands of the Maharaja."

Peter David rose to his feet.

"Mr Richardson," he said. "I'm sure you did not intend to be rude, but in Scotland we do not address gentlemen by their last names. It is Mr Small, or if you wish to be formal, Baillie Small. No. Let me finish. A Baillie is the equivalent of your London Alderman. Mr Small is a member of the Town Council and a magistrate. No doubt we are not as well off as you, but we did not rescue Bali and the emerald for a reward! And you *should* know that in the course of keeping Bali and the emerald safe, both Mr Small and myself have been assaulted and Mrs Small attacked in her own home. Finally your major thanks are due to little ragged boy who, with great courage, and knowing nothing of a reward, prevented Fizjames from murdering Mr Small and stealing the emerald and probably saved Bali from serious assault if not death."

Peter's voice had been rising during this speech. Bali had wakened and now stood in the doorway to the kitchen supported by Dod, who, though still little, did not look particularly ragged.

"Mr Richardson, I presume, Pleased to meet you," said Bali, extending his hand.

"Prince," said Richardson, taking the hand and making a slight bow. "I had no idea you had been so badly hurt."

"It is as Mr Small said, I cannot travel at present. But, even if I could, I have no intention of leaving Dundee and my new friends until Fizjames is captured."

"But Prince – your father ……….."

Bali held up his hand.

"Help me to a chair, Dod."

"Mr Richardson, I am very pleased that you are here. There are many things to be done which I am neither fit nor able to undertake. Firstly you will write to my father, by the first Company ship to leave for India, and tell him that I am safe and that the Emerald of Hanuman has been recovered. Tell him that I sustained a minor injury and that I will stay in Dundee until I am fully recovered. You need not worry him by mentioning that Fizjames is still at large. Next you can arrange for poor Mr Diprose's body to be taken to his family in Wiltshire. I presume the Company will pay all the expenses. Finally I need some money. Jasper was in charge of our finances and the police are looking after his valuables."

Poor Mr Richardson was reeling under the dual verbal assaults of Peter and Bali. John took the opportunity to suggest they begin again, and having accepted a glass of whisky Mr Richardson listened to the complete story. When John had finished, Richardson cleared his throat.

"I clearly owe you an apology," he said, nodding towards John and Peter. "You have both done more to assist the Prince and the Company than anyone could have expected."

"As for you," he continued, turning to Dod. "You are clearly an exceptional young man. The Company could use you! Now I think I should go. I have had a long and tiring journey. I will see you tomorrow when I have dealt with Mr Diprose's affairs."

Mr Richardson had kept a Hackney cab waiting outside the Smalls' close. He got in and directed the driver to return to the Royal Hotel. As the cab started, Dod jumped silently on to the back, as he, and most of the other Dundee urchins had done on many an occasion, and hitched a lift as far as the junction of the Nethergate and School Wynd, where he jumped off. He and Shadow, who had been running behind the cab, began the long walk up the hill while Mr Richardson carried on to his bed in the Royal Hotel.

Back at the Smalls' house John and Peter had a second dram.

"Not a bad fellow, in the end," said Peter.

"Well, you certainly put him in his place!" replied John.

"As did young Bali - the Company clearly thinks a lot of his father."

"I don't like it," said John, "but I think all we can do now is to wait for Fitzjames to make a move. I for one have Council work to do tomorrow – as well as a bakery to run!"

Chapter 15

In which Betsey makes a mistake and Dod takes charge

B etsey was bored. The children had been confined to the house for five days now. This was made even worse by the fact that Dod, who Betsey was beginning to think of as an honorary brother, could come and go as he pleased. John had patiently explained that firstly Dod was not his son and so he could not tell him what to do, secondly Dod's mother might be rather upset if her son was locked up in the Smalls' house and thirdly Dod had been effectively looking after himself for many years. None of this, however, made the time pass more quickly.

After dinner at midday, the house was quiet. John had gone to the Town House, Elizabeth was serving in the shop below. Bali and Elizabeth's mother were dozing. Bessie grabbed Alec.

"Lets get out o' here," she said. "I dinna ken how lang the menagerie's staying for – and I want tae see the elephant!"

"We canna gae oot," said Alec, "Faither said ………."

"Never mind what Faither said. We'll be back before him. Mither'll be in the shop till six and grannie'll be out for the count for a couple of oors. George can lock the door behind us. Naebody'll ken we've gone except the policeman, and he was telt tae keep people oot, not tae keep us in. Come on, Alec, yer no scared are you?"

Although he was a year older, Alec found it difficult to cross his sister. She organised the games and was usually the leader of their "gang". This occasion was no different and ten minutes later Bessie and Alec were out of the house and on their way to the Magdalene Green where the Fair been set up. The walked down the Hawkhill to the Sinderins, then along Perth Road before cutting down Taylors Lane. If they had looked behind them they might have noticed a tall man in a black coat with a hat pulled well over his face. If they had had Dod and Shadow with them, they would have been alerted by Shadow's growl. But they were on their own and just happy to be outside and so they saw nothing. The fair was not very busy on a Tuesday afternoon and many of the rides and stalls were closed. But the menagerie was open and they paid their penny each to go inside. It was not a very large menagerie, not like the ones which toured round

London, but the animals were exciting enough for the two children whose closest encounters had been in the pages of books. The elephant did not disappoint. It was a small Indian elephant, but they arrived just as it was being fed - picking up fruit and vegetables with its trunk.

"That's amazing," said Betsey. "You'd think it was an arm and no a nose!"

The pair of lionesses did what lions usually do in the afternoon and slept.

"They're just like a pair o' cats," said Alex, "Ye could probably stroke them."

"I wouldnae try that," said one of the menagerie men. "Look at their whiskers twitching. They're no' really asleep. If ye went in there they'd have ye fur their denner!"

The Bengal tiger was much better value – pacing back and forward in his cage, stopping occasionally to snarl at the people staring at him. There were a few other animals – funny stripy horses called zebras and a couple of wee kangaroos that the label on the cage said were wallabies and came from New Zealand. There was a small aviary with parakeets and a cockatoo – and an evil looking vulture.

"I'm going into the tent there tae look at the snakes," said Betsey to Alec who was mesmerised by a large Eagle Owl. "See you in there."

Two minutes later, Alec went into the snake tent but there was no sight of Betsey. He looked round the rest of the menagerie, even going behind some of the cages. Finally he ran round the whole fairground. After half an hour of fruitless searching he found a man who remembered a girl a bit like Betsey leaving with a tall man in a black coat.

All Alec could do was rush home. He ran straight into the shop where Elizabeth was serving and blurted out the whole story. Elizabeth immediately sent one of the apprentices to fetch John from the Town House. Leaving the other apprentice in charge she took Alec back up to the house to wait for his father to arrive. It was getting on for five o'clock by this time and Dod turned up, hoping for his tea, to find Elizabeth sitting in the dark and Alec sobbing in a corner. He immediately turned to Dod.

"He's taken Betsey – I'm sure it was him. I wish you and Faither had let him tak the dashed emerald when he came for it. None o' this would have happened!"

John arrived, and the whole story was told again. Then, just after the Old Steeple struck five, there was a knock on the door. The policeman propelled in a very small boy holding a letter.

"Ah was telt tae wait till the Steeple struck five afore I brocht this. Ah was telt I'd get a penny."

John grabbed the letter and tore it open.

"Its from Fizjames. He says he's got Betsey and he's taking her tae France or Holland. When he's there he'll tell us where to bring the emerald."

Dod knelt down and spoke to the small boy, who in the light of the obvious distress and anger the letter had caused, had started sobbing.

"When did he gie ye the letter, and where were ye?"

"Ah wuz doon at the docks and the Steeple had just gone three. He wuz an affy big man and he said Ah'd get a penny."

"Had he onyone wi' him – a wee girl?"

"Naw he was on his lane. Can ah go noo?"

"No wait a bit. We micht need ye tae tak anither message."

Dod pulled at John Small's sleeve to get his attention.

"Maister Sma'," he said. "He's got tae go by sea. I'm going tae see Captain Melville – he'll ken what tae dae."

"You, whit's yer name, come wi' me," he said to the boy who had at least stopped crying and was wiping his nose on his sleeve.

"Tam."

"Come wi' me then Tam. We're going back doon tae the docks. Ye can show me exactly where ye met the man."

And the two boys left.

Dod ran all the way to the docks with Shadow at his heels and wee Tam just about keeping up behind them. When he got to the *Oxalis* he rushed up the gangplank and shouted for Jim.

"I need tae see the Captain," he said. "Its urgent. Baillie Sma's dauchter Betsey has been kidnapped."

"He's at the Exchange," said Jim. "But ye'll hae tae argue wi' the man on the door. He's sent me aff afore when I tried tae speak tae the Captain."

"Stay here wi' Jim," he said to wee Tam. "I micht need ye tae tak a message when I've talked tae the Captain."

Dod ran to the Exchange Coffee House – it only took him a couple of minutes. Getting a message to the Captain was, however, more difficult. He approached the doorman.

"I've got an urgent message for Captain Melville from Baillie Small." he said.

This produced a grunt from the doorkeeper and a "We dinna want your type here!"

"I said it was urgent," said Dod but realising that argument would get him nowhere he nodded at the man and said "Guard" to Shadow, who immediately stood in front of him and bared her teeth. Dod nipped past him and into the main coffee room. He looked round and finally noticed the Captain at a table with three other men. He approached from behind Captain Melville and tapped him on the shoulder.

"Sorry tae bother you, Captain," he said, "but I've an affy important message frae Baillie Small. He needs you urgently."

"Gentlemen," said Melville, "I had better go and find out what this young man has to say." Turning to Dod he whispered, "This had better be important – I'm with my future father-in-law."

In the lobby the first thing the Captain noticed was the poor doorman pressed up against the wall by Shadow.

"Good grief – this had better be really important," he exclaimed,

"Baillie Small's dauchter, Betsey, has been kidnapped by yon Fizjames. He sent a note saying that they were going tae France or Holland. I think they're going by sea. You're the anely one who can help." All this said without taking a breath.

"Right," said the Captain, "I'll just go and tell my friends that I won't be back. Wait outside the door with your dog. You've frightened poor Peter half to death."

Dod stood just outside the door listening intently. He was worried that he might have overstepped the mark and lost the Captain's friendship, but he was reassured when he heard Melville saying, "Here's a half crown, Peter. Forget this ever happened, but if that boy ever comes with a message for me again, bring it in immediately."

They walked quickly back to the *Oxalis*. Dod told him the details of Betsey's abduction and what was in the letter. He then explained about his sighting of Fizjames with the man who he thought might be a sailor.

"Describe him," said the Captain.

"Fizjames is aboot six feet tall, so the man would be aboot five feet three or fower. He has long greasy grey hair sticking oot of woollen cap. Oh and I think he might have has a wee bit of a limp."

"I think I know who that might be," said Melville. They were now back at the ship. "Jim," run along the docks and see if Duncan Brown's boat is missing. If it is ask around and try to find out when it left and where it was going."

Captain Melville suddenly noticed the presence of a very dirty small boy.

"That's wee Tam." said Dod, "He brought the letter to Mr Small. I thought he could take a message to Mr David. We should let him know what's happened."

"Ah still hav'na got ma penny, and ma Ma'll be worried." piped up Tam.

Captain Melville searched in his pocket. "Here's tuppence," he said, "Now do what Dod here tells you."

"Whar dae ye bide," said Dod.

"Up the Hulltoon, in Ann Street."

"Can ye read numbers?"

"If ye write them in the dust there, ah kin recognise them."

Dod took a stick and traced 148 in the dust.

"Keep gaeing up the Hulltoon efter Ann Street, the right haund side, number 148. Ye want Mr David the builder. Tell him that Baillie Sma's dauchter has been kidnapped and that he's tae gae tae the Baillie's as soon as he can. He micht gie ye anither penny."

Jim returned.

"Ye were richt," he said. "Duncan took his boat oot at aboot half past three. Its ca'd the *Pride o' Arbroath*, by the way, although apparently there's nothing much tae be prood of. There were three people on board and he was heading across the Tay towards Buddon Ness. Oh and I got a description o' the boat – its no very weel painted and the sail's patched. Apparently abody kens Duncan's boat because of the black patch in the corner of his sail."

"Very good, Jim," said the Captain. "George, go back to the Smalls and tell them I'll be round in about an hour. We will leave at first light and I have some arrangements to make."

When Dod got back to the Smalls' house things had calmed down a little. Angus McLeod had been round and, although he had not been pleased at being kept in the dark about the emerald and the involvement of the East India Company, he had taken the abduction seriously and gone to alert all railway stations in Scotland. Alec had been sent to bed and John and Elizabeth were sitting talking.

"Captain Melville and Mr David will be round in a while," said Dod. "We ken who's boat Fizjames has hired and the Captain thinks we can catch it long before it gets tae France or wherever."

Elizabeth seemed unconvinced. Dod explained that according to the Captain, Duncan would not sail during the night and that the *Oxalis* could travel about twice as fast as a fishing boat. When Captain Melville came round about an hour later he explained in more detail.

"He can maybe do four knots if he is lucky, but his boat is not well maintained and he has to hug the coast. We can do ten knots and go further out to sea to catch the wind. It's the new moon in a couple of days so it's pitch dark as soon as the sun sets. Duncan started at about half past three and had about two, maybe three hours before it would be too dark. That means he probably put in at Crail, or thereabouts, to spend the night. Duncan won't want to go too far in his little boat. On the other hand Fizjames probably will not risk trying to catch a train in Scotland – his description will have been circulated to all the stations by now – so I would guess they are heading for Newcastle or another of the Northumberland ports. If he starts off at six in the morning he might make Dunbar by midday. If we leave at six we can be there about the same time. You'll be coming I expect, John; and you too Peter? I don't suppose we can leave young George, here, behind – but you will have to do as your told, ships are dangerous places."

Chapter 16

In which the "Oxalis" goes in pursuit

At six the next morning the *Oxalis* left its moorings. On board were: James Melville (Captain), Peter Sharp (mate) Malcolm Chisholm (seaman) Jim Mitchell (apprentice). John Small, Peter David, Dod Johnson, Shadow (dog) and Rodriguez (monkey). John had brought with him an ancient musket which he claimed his father had used in the Militia during the French wars. They sailed out of the Tay estuary, round Buddon Ness, past Fife Ness and then straight towards the Lothian coast. They all felt differently about the expedition. To the crew this was merely a job. Captain Melville, John and Peter were more worried. No-one could be sure that they would catch the fishing boat – indeed John was not entirely convinced that Fizjames had escaped that way – and no-one could predict what he would do when cornered. To Dod, who could not really believe that anyone, not even Fizjames, would really harm a little girl, this was an adventure. He started the voyage by feeding and then playing with Rodriguez. But monkeys, unlike dogs, eventually get tired of humans. Rodriguez clearly wanted out on deck so, after asking the Captain if this was permitted, he opened the cabin door and let the monkey out. After checking out the whole ship and catching a few fleas from Shadow, Rodriguez retired to the Crow' Nest.

Dod was scanning the shore as they approached North Berwick.

"Yon's a funny hill sticking oot there, affy like the Dundee Law," said Dod, who unsurprisingly was not staying quiet, although he was more or less doing what he was told.

"That's Berwick Law," said Jim, "and yer richt, it does look a bit like the Law in Dundee. Yon great rock in the sea there's ca'd the Bass Rock. Look ower there, tae yer left, and ye can see a braw castle sticking oot intae the sea too – that's Tantallon."

When they got to Dunbar, Captain Melville slackened the sail and anchored about half a mile off shore.

"Here, George," said the Captain. "This will keep you occupied. Take my telescope. Look carefully at every sail. We're looking for one with a black patch."

For the next half hour Dod scanned the waters between the ship and the coast, studying every sail carefully – but no sign of one with a patch. John was getting frustrated.

"Are ye sure he's no' ahead of us, James. Should we no' just keep going."

"I'm fairly sure we will have overtaken him," said the Captain. "Give it another half hour, and if he hasn't appeared we'll carry on for a bit more"

But just before the time was up there was a yell from Dod.

"There it is. Coming down the coast."

The Captain grabbed the telescope.

"Yes, you're right. That's Duncan Brown's boat. Up sail, we'll get well ahead of him, tack round and approach from the south. That way we can block his passage.

The *Pride o' Arbroath* was keeping as close to the coast as it was safe to do and making a steady four knots, Duncan saw a ship coming towards them on the port side. He peered at it through narrowed eyes and got a shock when eventually he was able to make out its name.

"That's the *Oxalis*", said Duncan. "Captain Melville frae Dundee. I wonder what he's daeing here. He must be coming back frae Newcastle or the like."

A minute later the *Oxalis* swung to starboard right in the path of Duncan's little boat causing him to swing the tiller round so that the ship and the fishing boat bumped into each other side to side. Fizjames got to his feet and looked up at the *Oxalis*. There he saw John Small, who he recognised, pointing a musket at him, two men who he did not recognise and, of course, Dod.

"Why not?" he thought. "He's probably brought his dammed dog as well to make up the party."

Fizjames grabbed Betsey and held her in front of him with his left hand. He slowly drew a pistol out of his waistband while keeping his eyes firmly fixed on John's musket.

"Put that ancient thing down," he said. "You'll more likely to hit your daughter than me."

He surveyed the four faces looking at him.

"I think I still hold the winning card," he said. "Just hand over the emerald and you can have this back." With this he gave Betsey a shake.

Fizjames then made a fatal mistake.

"I think I'll have your ship, Captain. It will be much more comfortable than this pathetic little thing," and he raised his pistol and pointed it directly at Captain Melville.

Fizjames saw a blur coming towards him and then felt a searing pain as Rodriguez jumped onto his head and sank his teeth into his right ear. Not to be outdone by this strange creature which her master had unaccountably taken a liking to, Shadow leaped on board the fishing boat and bit Fizjames hard on the ankle. She was followed by Dod, who jumped down and began to untie the ropes tying Betsey's wrists and ankles. Finally Captain Melville, who was by far the youngest of the three men, boarded the *Pride*, and formally arrested Fizjames in the name of the Queen.

A ladder was lowered and Fizjames, his hands now bound behind him, was helped to climb up. He was followed by Betsey and Dod, then Duncan, protesting all the time that he knew nothing about a kidnapping.

"He said it was his ain dauchter and he was stealin' her awa' frae her mither!" he said.

"If you believe that you'll believe anything," said the Captain bringing up the rear. A short bark reminded them that Shadow was still on the fishing boat. Jumping down had been easy, but she needed help to get back up onto the ship. Rodriguez was already back on his favourite place in the rigging. Betsey was none the worse for her experience, but was naturally worried about her father's reaction to her unauthorised visit to the menagerie. She need not have worried, he was so pleased to have her back unharmed that the reason she was able to be kidnapped in the first place was forgotten. The fishing boat was tied behind the *Oxalis* and they went into the port at Dunbar. There John wrote a short letter to Elizabeth telling her that Betsey was fine and that they would be back tomorrow. Fizjames, hands tied behind his back, was also taken ashore to have his badly bitten ear sewn up. When they returned to the ship he was locked in one of the cabins. As John closed the door he turned to Fizjames and said, "You really did underestimate us, didn't you. Beaten by an eleven year old boy, a dog and a monkey. You'll have lot to think about as you wait for your trial!" Duncan was still on deck, looking very scared.

"We should decide what to do about him before we get back to Dundee," said Melville, indicating the fisherman.

"I don't think we need bother about the wee nyaff," said John.

"Were going tae let ye aff this time," he continued. "But if you ever come up before the Baillies at Dundee in the future for anything at all, it'll be the jail for you!"

"Fizjames is more difficult. The only witness to Diprose's murder is Bali. I know that Richardson is desperate to get him back to his father as soon as he can travel and the Assizes might be three or even six months from now. However we can easily get him for attempted murder and abduction of a minor – there are plenty of witnesses for those two crimes. They should be enough to get him transportation for life."

"Aye," said Peter. "If we offer to drop the murder charge he might plead guilty to the others and save everyone a bit of trouble – I'm sure you can square it with Angus."

They left Dunbar and sailed back across the Firth of Forth,

"We'll dock at Anstruther for the night," said the Captain. "I know a good inn where you, Peter and Betsey can sleep. I presume you, turning to Dod, would rather sleep on board."

"Oh yes, please, Captain," said Dod. "I can sleep next tae Jim and learn whit its like tae be a real sailor."

Next morning they sailed from Anstruther and were soon back in the William IV Dock in Dundee. As John had said, Duncan was released and given his boat back.

"I don't think he'll be breaking any laws soon," said Peter.

Fizjames was taken to the prison in Bell Street where Angus formally charged him with the attempted murder of "ane o' the Baillies o' the toon – one John Small", of "brakin' intae the Baillie' hoose tae the great fear o' his wife Elizabeth", of "paying twa ruffians tae assault Peter David, Deacon o' the Masons" and finally of "abducting a minor, one Betsey Small, wi' the intention o' carrying her aff furth o' the Kingdom". He took John's advice and offered to drop the murder charge if Fizjames admitted to all these other charges. John took Betsey home to be reunited with her mother and siblings. Alec, who still felt responsible for her kidnapping, was particularly pleased to see her safe and well. And Dod went home to his mother. He had told her only that he was going on a short trip with Captain Melville, so she had no idea that he might have been in danger. Her main concern was that he had not earned much money in the last week.

Chapter 17

In which the Smalls hold a party

During the next week, things gradually got back to normal. Bali slowly recovered his strength and eventually was able to go out. He was usually accompanied by Dod and by Henry Ogilvie, who had become quite a friend. Henry had remembered that Bali was a vegetarian and thinking that "home cooking" might help his recovery he had turned up at the Smalls' house with a young lascar from the docks who showed Elizabeth how to cook a "curry".

"I can dae three Indian dishes now," she said to one of her neighbours. "One is like a stew of vegetables and tomatoes, wi' some spices, one is just spicy thick lentil soup – so that was no problem, and the third is affy like potato fritters, except ye put a bit spice in the batter and use caulifloor or onions – they're ca'ed ba-gees!"

The boys went down to the harbour to see Captain Melville and Jim, and of course, Rodriguez and Dod finally got to see his elephant when the whole Small family accompanied by Bali, Dod, Henry and Willie David went to the menagerie. Betsey conveniently forgot the problems her first visit had caused and showed them round as if she owned the place. The day the three boys climbed to the top of the Law, John wrote to Mr Richardson, who had returned to London, to tell him that Bali was fully recovered and could travel home.

A week later John organised a large gathering in his house. Nearly everyone who had been remotely involved in the "Fizjames affair" or the "Case of the Emerald of Hanuman", as it had variously become known, was invited. Elizabeth wrote personally to Jeannie to invite her. She was very aware that Dod had been spending a great deal of time with the Smalls and suspected Jeannie might resent this. She was not at all sure that Jeannie would come if invited only by Dod. She asked Dod what his mother called herself and confirmed that she, in common with many women in her position, used Mrs and Dod's father's name.

Dear Mrs Johnson, she wrote, This Saturday we are having a small gathering at tea time to say farewell to our Indian guest, Bali, and to celebrate the satisfactory conclusion of a difficult and dangerous case in which your boy Dod has been heavily involved. I am very aware that Dod has spent too much time away from you over the last two weeks, but as you probably know, but for him Mr Small would have been badly injured or worse. Dod has mentioned you often and Mr Small and I would love to meet you. Mr David and Isabella will also be attending. Elizabeth Small.

And so on the Saturday evening a large gathering began to assemble at the Smalls' house. By five o'clock the table in the large kitchen had been laid with all the usual festive foods: a boiled ham, potted hough, potted chicken, some curry and dahl for Bali, bread, butter, pickles, scones, jam and cakes – the whole selection of cakes for which John Allan Small, baker, was famous. The four Small children, and Henry Ogilvie who had been there most of the day, were all dressed in their Sunday best and fidgeted about while waiting for the guests to arrive. Bali had dressed in his Indian clothes for the occasion.

Dod had, of course, been there earlier but at three o'clock Elizabeth grabbed him and said, "Go home now. Ye can't expect your mother to come here on her ain. In fact you can't expect her tae walk here. Here's a shilling – you can get a Hackney Cab. Oh, and leave yer dug here. She'll be fine with Betsey and the rest of the children. Yer mother won't be happy if there's a dug running behind the cab!"

So Dod went home where he found Jeannie getting into her "Kirk claese" and generally panicking.

"Dinna worry mither," he said. "They're a' affy couthy fowk. Ye'll like Mistress Sma' and ye ken Mistress Davie tae nod tae in the street."

Hansom cabs were few and far between on the Hilltown so they walked together down the hill to the Wellgate where they picked one up just outside Mr Niven's shop.

Back at the Smalls' house the guests were assembling. The Davids were first to arrive, Isabella wishing to get there early to give Elizabeth a hand to set the table. Captain Melville turned up with a scrubbed and somewhat embarrassed Jim in tow. Careful scrutiny of Jim's trousers suggested that they may have belonged originally to the Captain and had been shortened at the leg.

"Guid afternain Mistress Small. Thank you for inviting me, but Ah'm nae sure why I'm here."

"You'll find out soon," said the Captain and Elizabeth in unison.

Exceptionally, for this occasion the Captain had brought Rodriguez, who with a collar round his neck and a chain firmly grasped in Jim's hand, had travelled on the boy's shoulder. Elizabeth peered at the monkey suspiciously.

"Well you did say that everyone concerned in the affair could come," James laughed. "And I don't think George would have forgiven me had I forgotten Rodriguez! He *is house-trained* by the way."

Dod and his mother arrived and Jeannie was whisked into the kitchen by Elizabeth while Dod joined the over-excited children and Shadow who, as usual, greeted him as if he had been away for a week. Elizabeth took Jeannie to one side.

"I jist thoch I'd let ye know that there's no need tae be embarrassed in this hoose aboot yer no being married. John's sister Jean, who lives in Lochee, has twa sons by twa different faithers. Baith men promised tae marry her and baith ran aff. I ken the Kirk aye blames the woman but we know it's usually the man, or his faimily's fault."

The final arrival was Mr Richardson who had taken a cab from the Royal Hotel where he was re-installed.

Everyone now joined the three women in the kitchen and, after John had said grace, the demolition of the feast commenced. Dod had learnt a lot about "manners" during the last couple of weeks and astonished his mother by delicately sipping his tea and not wolfing down his food. She also noticed, however, that his new manners did not extend to refraining from feeding Shadow under the table. Rodriguez, fortunately, had been fed before leaving and, having been let off the chain, accepted an apple and retreated to the top of the kitchen press. The meal finished, John announced that they would all go through to the front room, where Mr Richardson and Bali had something to say.

The front room, which like all front rooms at that time, was used only for very special occasions was at the side of the house overlooking the quieter Hunter Street. To take the November chill off the air there had been a fire burning since early morning and the gas lights were all turned up brightly. They all settled down - the adults on the settle and various chairs, the children on the floor. Rodriguez, who could not be safely left in the kitchen, decided to settle down next to Shadow and from time to time gave her fur a stroke. Shadow, for her part, had decided that the strange creature was probably a kind of puppy and gave it an occasional lick. Betsey's cat, who had decided that she liked monkeys even less than dogs, jumped on Elizabeth's lap and her purr was soon competing with the soft crackling of the fire as background noise.

Chapter 18

In which Dod's life is changed

Mr Richardson stood up which, Dod observed to himself, did not make much difference to his height. Dod was trying to remember who Mr Richardson reminded him of, and had just decided that it was Mr Pickwick in one of Mr Dickens' stories, when he began to speak.

"Ladies and Gentlemen," he began. "I should start by explaining the background to this affair because many of you only know about the effect it has had on your lives here in Dundee. Prince Bali's father is the Maharaja, the ruler, of a small kingdom in India. Small, but of great strategic importance to the East India Company, of whom I am a representative. As part of our involvement we supplied the Maharaja with a small number of Company troops, one of whom was unfortunately Captain Fizjames. As you know, Fizjames stole an emerald from the principal temple, the Temple of Hanuman, in the Maharaja's capital, killing two priests. This, of course, was hugely embarrassing to the Company. It also put the Maharaja in a very difficult position. If the emerald could not be recovered, his enemies, who resent the Company's influence, would be strengthened. Fizjames escaped on a jute boat disguised as a lascar. Prince Bali and one of the Company's best men, Jasper Diprose, overtook him by sailing on a British Navy frigate. Unfortunately we all underestimated Fizjames and, but for the efforts of people in this room, he would have escaped with the jewel and the Prince might possibly have been killed." As he spoke he nodded towards John, Peter, Captain Melrose and, finally, Dod. John then took a small packet out of his waistcoat pocket, unwrapped it, held the emerald up in front of one of the gaslights and then presented it to Bali. Apart from Bali, the only people in the room who had seen the jewel were John, Peter and the Captain, and then only fleetingly, and the effect of the gem flashing in the light was startling. ………

Mr Richardson continued, "The Company offered a reward for the retrieval of the emerald and the capture of Fizjames. Mr Small and Mr David have declined to accept the reward but, after discussions with them, we have decided to give each of the young people in this room a small reward of ten guineas."

Captain Melville turned to Jim, "Now you know why you're here!"

"But Ah didnae dae onything except ma joab," exclaimed Jim.

"Sometimes in this life," said the Captain, almost to himself. "It is enough to be in the right place, at the right time and just do your job. Pardon me. Please continue Mr Richardson."

"Captain Melville has also refused a reward. However we understand you are about to be married and you will not refuse a wedding present of twenty five guineas from the Company. And we insist on paying you for the hire of your ship for two days."

Captain Melville stood up and bowed to Mr Richardson.

"Now we turn to young George, or Dod as I believe you are commonly known. I must confess when I first came here I was astonished at the fact that the case was being pursued by a pair of tradesmen and not the police. Indeed, and he went even redder, I was rather rude to Mr Small and Mr David, for which I have apologised. I was even more astonished by the involvement of an eleven year old boy, and one who, frankly, and he began to splutter, almost lived on the street. However," he continued, stretching to his full height and looking directly at Dod, "I have come to realise that you have rather remarkable qualities. Not only are you brave, but you seem to be capable of assessing a situation and taking immediate action."

John Small interjected, "Mr Richardson is referring to the time when you rushed and got Captain Melville while I was just sitting here wondering what should be done. If it hadn't been for your quick thinking Betsey might be in Holland by now."

"Anyway," said Mr Richardson. "We have discussed what reward you should have. Mr Small and Mr David originally intended that one of them could offer you an apprenticeship – but we somehow thought you did not really want to be a baker or a mason. I did consider that you might like to go to sea."

"Aye, I might like that fine," said Dod, with a vague feeling that perhaps he should have been consulted, but knowing perfectly well that adults usually thought they knew best."

"But then," said Mr Richardson. "I had a better idea. I went to see your mother."

"You whit?" exclaimed Dod.

"I went to see your mother," continued Richardson, unperturbed. "And she told me that you have always wanted to go to school. So, if you agree, we will pay all expenses, including a living allowance of ten pounds a year, for you to attend the Public Seminaries until you are sixteen. And," he continued, holding up his hand to stop Dod interjecting, "again if you wish it and if you do well enough I will suggest that the Governors recommend you be employed as a writer or a cadet in the East India Company when you leave school."

For the second time in his life, Dod was speechless.

Finally, realising that they were all waiting for him to speak, he said, "Thank you very much Mr Richardson, I would very much like to go to school," and then, becoming more and more excited, "If I join the Company will I get tae go tae India and see elephants and tigers?".

"If you want to, if you pass the examinations and if I can persuade the Governors. The Maharaja will be helpful here. And you don't have to decide for five years."

Dod turned to Willie David.

"Will I manage at school," he asked. "I'm a bit late tae start."

"Ye'll manage fine," said Willie. "You can read and write as well as me. You could get extra lessons in mathematics and languages from Mr Lindsay – mind we met him the other day – he's a very good teacher."

Bali now stood up, "That reward was from the Company – there is another from my father and myself."

He turned towards the animals which were almost asleep in front of the fire.

"Rodriguez!"

The monkey looked up.

Bali said something in Hindi and, although not an Indian monkey, Rodriguez clearly understood the tone and went over to Bali. Bali produced something from his pocket, gave it to Rodriguez, and said something else in Hindi, this time pointing at Dod. The monkey looked at Bali, looked at Dod, then looked at the Captain who also pointed at Dod. So Rodriguez went up to the boy and held out the object Bali had given him.

"It is only fit," he said, "that the one who saved the Emerald of Hanuman should receive his reward from an incarnation of Hanuman, albeit one from another continent. Dod, I install you as a member of the Order of the Gold Elephant – for exceptional service to our country."

The object which Rodriguez had handed over was a beautifully crafted gold elephant, about two inches long with a small ruby for an eye, hanging on a gold chain.

"And it comes," said Bali, "taking a heavy bag from under his chair where it had remained unnoticed, "with a small sum of money – a thousand silver rupees."

Mr Richardson's jaw literally fell open. Before he could say a word, Bali continued, "Not a great sum of money for saving a kingdom."

Captain Melville broke the silence. "Do you want to buy the *Oxalis*? I'll let you have it for a good price! And I'll throw in Jim and the monkey for good measure!" Dod correctly assumed this was a joke and started laughing. John produced glasses and poured whisky for the men, sherry for the ladies (although Jeannie would have preferred whisky) and Elizabeth's home made lemonade for the children.

"A toast," he said. "To Dod, who will soon have a new life, and to a safe voyage home for our new friend Bali."

The conversation which ensued was mainly about how to spend (or generally not to spend) the money which the children had received. The Small children were informed that they could spend the ten shillings on toys and such if they wanted, but the ten pounds was going into the Bank. The Captain was talking to Jim in a corner.

"I can't tell you what to do with your money, but here's my advice. Spend the ten shillings – buy your mother and sister something nice for Christmas. But put the ten pounds in the Bank. Leave it till you get your Master's ticket – maybe in about twenty years time – and by then your ten pounds will be worth about eighteen pounds. With that you can buy a quarter share in a schooner. There's a world of difference between being a Captain who is working for owners and a Captain who also is an owner."

Henry was talking to Mr Small.

"I want to thank you for letting me be a part of this," he said. "I'm going back to India with Bali as a sort of companion or advisor. Mr Richardson is happy that he won't be travelling on his own. I'm going to stay for a year and see how I like it."

Dod was still not quite sure what a thousand rupees was worth, but he was sure from the general conversation that it would end up in the Bank as well. He finally got to the Captain who did a rough calculation in his head.

"A thousand rupees is a bit more than two hundred pounds. It should bring in about six pounds a year, or if you leave it till you are eighteen, about fifty pounds."

"That's an affy lot o' money," said Dod.

"Don't worry," said Captain Melville. "Its an affy expensive world we live in!"

Chapter 19

In which Wee Tam gets a bath and acquires a business

Next day, as Dod came out of the entry connecting his tenement to the Hilltown, he noticed a small figure trying to look inconspicuous.

"Hullo, Dod," it said. "That's a braw dug ye've got."

"Guid mornin' Tam," replied Dod. "I don't expect this is a coincidence." Word had already got around that Dod had got a reward, although the exact amount had been kept secret. Tam began to stroke Shadow.

"Ah dinna suppose ye'll be runnin' ony mair messages noo ye're famous. And ah wis good at delivering they twa the ither day. Ah took the one tae Mr Sma' "exactly when the Steeple struck five" and ah fund Mr Davie's hoose fur you."

Dod felt a surge of relief. Tam wanted his former business, not a handout. This he could do.

"Aye well Tam, I suppose I could introduce ye to a few people, Ye already ken Mr David and Baillie Sma', although he might take some persuading to use you. But we'll hae tae get ye a bit cleaner if ye want tae succeed. Ye're affy claerty and fowk dinna like claerty wee boys in their hooses or their places o' business."

"But Dod, its ower cald tae wash in the winter. Ah gae and hae a dook in the river maist weeks in the summer, but noo…."

"We'll go back tae my hoose and pick up the claese I was wearing before Mistress Sma' gave me the ones I'm wearing noo, they'll jist aboot fit ye, and then we'll gae doon tae the docks and get ye clean."

"The docks!" cried Tam. "Ah'm no jumpin' in the docks!"

"Te daft wee gowk, have ye no heard o' the Public Baths next tae the Earl Grey. Ye get a guid hot bath for a ha'penny – I'll pey. I need a bath myself anyway before I get some new claese for gaein' tae skale."

They went back to Dod's room where his old clothes were wrapped in old newspapers and tied up with string. On the way down to the docks they passed Mr Niven's shop.

"Mr Niven," said Dod. "This is Tam. He'll be taking over from me running messages. I hope you can use him. And dinna worry, I'm just going tae get him cleaned up."

An hour later they emerged from the baths. Despite his initial misgivings, Tam enjoyed splashing about in hot water and had to be more or less thrown out by the attendant. As they were almost there Dod could not resist a quick visit to the *Oxalis* to give Rodriguez an apple, which resulted in open-mouthed staring and cap-clutching from Tam. The visit was, however, short as the ship was preparing to leave for the Baltic. As they walked back Dod introduced Tam to several of his regulars: Mr Sherriff the builder, Mr Beatts, the auctioneer, an advocate and a couple of Jute Brokers. He also gave Tam some advice.

"Keep yersel clean, but not too weel dressed – ye'll get mair money if fowk feel sorry fur you. Learn tae talk English and speak tae people in the same language that they speak tae you. I dinna mean that you imitate them mind, but ye canna talk broad Scotch tae yon advocate, or to a Doctor but ye needna speak English tae the likes of Mr Niven or Mr Davie."

"Hoo dae ah learn tae speak English," asked Tam.

"Ye'll hae tae learn tae read," replied Dod. "It maks ye much mair use as a messenger onyway. Ah suppose Ah'll hae tae dae that tae. Go and try yer luck now wi' Mr Davie, Ah'll see ye the morn and gie ye yer first lesson."

Chapter 20

In which Dod gets a surprise visitor

Two weeks later Dod was sitting in the kitchen of the new house which Jeannie and he had rented. It was a great improvement on their previous accommodation, with three rooms and a kitchen. There was no inside toilet, these were still very uncommon, but there was one on the landing which they only shared with one other family. Most importantly for Dod, it was lit by gas which made reading much more pleasant than it had been by candle light. It was five o'clock and he was in his new clothes doing some homework. He would not start at the Seminaries till January, but in the meantime he had taken Willie's advice and was getting lessons in mathematics from Mr Lindsay. Jeannie had left the mill and had agreed to help out in the Smalls' shop till Elizabeth had her baby. Dod had just finished a problem in geometry when there was a knock on the door.

"Come in, its no locked."

The man who entered looked slightly familiar to Dod, but he couldn't quite place him.

"George?" the man said.

"Aye," said Dod, "But only Captain Melville ca's me that. Who are you?"

The man sat down heavily on one of the kitchen chairs.

"I'm your father, George. I'm Tom Johnson."

Dod looked at him carefully.

"Aye, you could be. There's a photograph that my mither kept of my faither when he was aboot eighteen. Ye do look like him. Why have ye come now. efter a' these years?"

"It's a long story, but I can make it short. My father sent me away to my uncle's farm as soon as he found out about my relationship with your mother. I was there for six years, and, before you ask, I did come back to Kinfauns from time to time and I did see you as a toddler. But when I'd been away about five years I met a girl and married her. I made the mistake of telling my father that we wanted to adopt you and, as you know, he sent you away. He was a very hard man. After he died I tried to find you and your mother, but no-one knew where you lived. Then I read all about you in the *Advertiser*, and here I am."

Dod looked thoughtful.

"My mither will be pleased tae see you," he said

"*You* don't seem so sure."

"If you'd come a year or two ago, or even a month ago, when we were living in a single end and mither was in the factory, I'd have been really happy. But a lot's happened recently. I've found three faithers, and a family. I'm to start school in January. I'm known roond the toun. Ah'm a real Dundonian now."

Just then Jeannie returned from her work at the Smalls' shop. She could hardly believe her eyes when she saw Tom and Dod looking at each other over the kitchen table.

"Tom," she exclaimed. "Whit are you daeing here?"

Tom gave her the same explanation he had given to Dod and then added that his wife had died last year leaving him with a three year old girl.

"You've got a little sister," he said to Dod.

Dod sat in silence for a minute or two and then said, "I'll leave you twa alane for a bit. I need tae ask someone something."

When Dod returned a couple of hours later Jeannie and Tom were still talking, their hands touching across the table.

"Tom has asked us tae gae and live on the ferm, Dod, but Ah'm no share, what do you think?"

Dod looked at his feet.

"Dae ye still love him," he mumbled.

"Aye," said Jeannie. "Ah think I do."

"Weel," said Dod. "I'll tell you what I think. You should stay here till Mistress Small can start back at the shop – ye owe her that. Maybe go and visit the farm and see how you feel. It'll be Christmas soon – we could spend it on the farm and I can meet my wee sister. If you really want tae go back and marry ma faither, Ah'll be happy for ye. As for me – I'm staying in Dundee."

Jeannie was about to interrupt him, but he continued.

"If ah lived on the ferm and went tae school in Perth Ah'd hae tae lodge wi' a family during the week. Ah'd rather stay here and lodge wi' the Baillie and Mrs Small. I can visit you maist weekends - there's a Friday night train tae Perth that stops at Kinfauns. I'll spend next summer with ye on the ferm, except for a week or two when the Captain has promised tae tak me for a trip on the *Oxalis*, and see how I like it. But it'll tak a while tae get used tae havin' a faither."

Chapter 21

The end

And that is where we have to leave Dod and his friends. How will Henry get on in India? Will Wee Tam make a go of the message business? Will Jeannie and Thomas marry? And will Dod........? Well of course he will. Whatever he decides to do will work out. I can't see him on the farm – but I might be wrong. Maybe we will visit him again in a while and find out!

Author's note

The story is set in November 1849. John Allan Small, Peter David and Captain James Whitton Melville were real people who lived and worked at the places and in the jobs which I describe. John Small was a Councillor, but not a Baillie. I have promoted him to give him more influence in the town (especially with the police). Mr Niven, Mrs Keillor, the Small's children, Willie David, James Bowman Lindsay and, of course, William MacGonigal are also all real, although I have sometimes changed the ages a little. This is, however, a work of fiction, and, as far as I know none of the above were involved in the recovery of an emerald.

Dod, his family, all the East India Company men, Bali, Jim, Wee Tam, Shadow, Rodriguez and sundry minor characters are invented, although Dod's back story is not unusual.

A word about the language. Some will wonder why the characters speak a fairly standard East Coast Scots and not in the Dundee (or Dundonesion as it is often called) dialect. (For those who are not familiar with this, it is characterised by the phrase Eh hud a peh fur ma dehnner *ie* a very hard eh for e or i). The reason I have done this is because I am fairly sure that in 1849 the late 19th century Dundee dialect had not yet developed. The expansion of Dundee had hardly begun. There had been little immigration from the Highlands or Ireland, and most importantly, the large spinning and weaving factories were just being built. I believe that the hardening of the Dundee vowels is largely due to having to shout over the noise of the looms. Just try asking for a pie when you can hardly hear yourself speak – then try peh. At least that's my theory and since there are no recordings from 1849 ....

I have also tried to make people speak as they would naturally. We are all aware that there is a "home" language and a "school" language. We know from the minutes of the Bakers' and Masons' Guilds that they could write in correct English. I suspect that most reasonably educated people could flip between English and Scots depending on who they were speaking to. I have tried to do this.

Printed in Poland
by Amazon Fulfillment
Poland Sp. z o.o., Wrocław